Reviews of the *BlackStar Ops Group* Series

Sandra L S

5.0 out of 5 stars

Reviewed in the United States on June 5, 201.

Verified Purchase

The latest book in BlackStar group is another winner for TC Miller. Each page has real sounding characters. Fast action keeps you glued to the story. Details on locations and ops from the good guys keeps the story fresh and real. Waiting on next book. Well done TC.

Me Me 518

5.0 out of 5 stars <u>This book is a page turner. Mr. Miller ...</u>

Reviewed in the United States on July 31, 2016

Verified Purchase

This book is a page turner. Mr. Miller is very knowledgeable in his writing and the characters interaction is spellbinding. You can not go wrong with this series of books. Looking forward to the next book.

Robert Enzenauer

5.0 out of 5 stars <u>A GREAT Military Action-Terrorist-Thriller</u>

Reviewed in the United States on October 3, 2016

WOW!!!! I really like this book. I have now read Volume 2 and Volume 3, and am 1/2 way through BlackJack Bomber. Miller's extensive military experience is evident in his vivid descriptions of units and unit actions. The pace of the plot is fast moving. The story of foreign spies and stolen nuclear weapons is right out of possible conflicts with the new Putin-led Russia after the "ReSet". Add to the international terrorists some kidnapping and blackmail - and the "bad guys" are about as evil as one can get. Most of the action takes place in my home state of Colorado, and I really like his attention to the details of his Colorado scenes. The final battle sequence between the "good guys" and the bad guys is truly remarkable. And without telling any plot details that would ruin the story for the prospective reader, Miller's novel is a very good, and the "good guys" win. Strong Work Miller!!

sandra toney

5.0 out of 5 stars <u>A fascinating adventure with more twists and curves than a country road</u>

Reviewed in the United States on November 12, 2019

I met T.C. Miller in Branson over the Veteran's Day holiday, 2019. When I spoke to him about this book, he said he had been visited by a gentleman wearing dark aviator glasses asking how he had so many facts correct about the highly secretive Cheyenne Mountain complex. Yes, the book is that good as the story continues with the attempt to locate stolen nukes by a special team. Miller adds personal knowledge from his years in the Air Force to his vivid imagination to create dialog that flows well and is spot on in terms of what you would expect from military personnel.

Jeffrey Miller

4.0 out of 5 stars <u>Miller does not disappoint with this third book in the BlackStar Ops series</u>

Reviewed in the United States on November 2, 2016

Verified Purchase

I'm a big fan of espionage thrillers and T.C. Miller does not disappoint with this third book in the BlackStar Ops series, BlackStar Mountain. Miller tells a good story and knows how to keep a reader riveted from one page to the next. If you like your reading fast and suspenseful, I highly recommend this book or the other books in the series.

Lee

5.0 out of 5 stars <u>Awesome!!</u>

Reviewed in the United States on December 5, 2017

Love his books!!

J. Thebige

5.0 out of 5 stars <u>Excellent third book in the series!</u>

Reviewed in the United States on December 29, 2017

Verified Purchase

The Third book in this series By now you have really learned all the characters and have favorites as this next in the series unfolds. As with the other two books an engaging read. You will find spots leaving you shocked or scratching your head. Personally the room described in the mountain side was fascinating. The end of this book makes you really want to see where T.C. takes the lives of his characters.

Thoughts on the series I typically read Christian adventure books, and westerns, not usually Military related mysteries. However, this series written by T.C. Miller really changed that for me. They are very well written as I have said with lots of detail and action that keeps the reader interested. As well as the fact they are a clean read. Leaving out the intimate scenes which are not necessary to the story. Personally my favorite characters were Joanna, Nora and Bart. The Glossary is also very helpful for someone without any military background. Overall a wonderful series which I will read over and over again! Excited to read the next in the series to see what happens next.

BLACKSTAR

DC

Award-Winning Author

Tc Miller and JA Schrock

Author T.c. Miller

T.c. formulated the plot for his debut novel, *BlackStar Bomber,* while stationed at Mather Air Force Base, California. His love of hiking and camping along the California coast provided the background for his second book, *Black Star Bay.* Six years of living in Colorado inspired *Black Star Mountain* and *BlackStar Enigma.* His lifelong study of Hakkoryu Jujitsu added elements to all his books.

He was the 2017 *Author of the Year* for the Rose State College Symposium for Writers.

His email is tc@tcmillerauthor.com, and his FaceBook page is T.c. Miller Author.

Author J.A. Schrock

J.A. retired from the United States Air Force as a Chief Master Sergeant after serving twenty-nine years, first active and then Air National Guard. He deployed five times to the Middle East, and twice stateside. He is the recipient of numerous medals, including Meritorious Service, Global War on Terrorism, Air Reserve Meritorious Service, National Defense Service Medals, and Armed Forces Reserve Medal w/Silver Hourglass & 3-M Devices. He also received the Indiana Overseas Ribbon and the Indiana OCONUS Ribbons.

Schrock also retired from the Goshen Indiana Police Department after serving his community for over thirty-five years. Additional duties included being the SCUBA Rescue and Recovery Team Supervisor, Honor Guard Instructor Team, and the M-14 Patrol Rifle team. He received the Law Enforcement Medal of Honor, Combat Cross, and Outstanding Unit Awards.

Schrock is a Goshen Police Department Reserve Officer, including serving on the Honor Guard. He also is a member of the Elkhart County Dive Team.

His FaceBook author page is J.A. Schrock Author.

Dedication and Acknowledgment

T.c. Miller

This book is dedicated to fans who encouraged me over the years to keep the story going. Your support is genuinely appreciated.

This book and all previous work have enjoyed the patience and input of my wife, J.K. Miller.

Ken Farmer and Buck Stienke of *Timber Creek Press* helped launch my career as a novelist.

William Bernhardt provided valuable insight and helped me grow as a writer through seminars at *The Writer's Colony* in Eureka Springs, Arkansas, and his annual writing conferences.

Jeff Schrock shared his experience in law enforcement, and I treasure his friendship of nearly forty years, to the extent that I asked him to co-write this book.

Mike Beckom lent his considerable commercial art expertise through his company, *MB Designs*.

I appreciate the support and encouragement of the *McLoud Area Writer's Group,* especially Glenda Kuhn

J.A. Schrock

This book, or at least my part of it, is based on the encouragement of T.c. Miller, without whom I would not have written anything more than a shopping list. I have learned more than I could have imagined.

Retired and now deceased Brigadier General William Reiff was also an inspiration who mentored me to become more than the sum of what I was.

More than thirty-five years on the Goshen Police Department, and the men and women who I had the privilege of working with, gave me the knowledge and experience I drew from in writing this book, as well as the nearly thirty years in the US Air Force and Air National Guard. To all of them, I say thank you.

The BlackStar Ops Group Series

Written by T.c. Miller:

BlackStar Bomber

BlackStar Bay

BlackStar Mountain

BlackStar Enigma

Written by T.c. Miller and J.A. Schrock:

BlackStar DC

BlackStar Consortium (To be released Fall of 2022)

Published by:
Winter Oak Studio, LLC
www.tcmillerauthor.com
tc@tcmillerauthor.com
FaceBook: T.c. Miller Author

Winter Oak Studio is the owner of this material.
First Publication date: February 22, 2022
ISBN-13: 979-8-9857344-1-6

Glossary

10-50PI	Vehicle accident with injuries
Alert Pad	Facility on where aircraft are parked for immediate response missions.
APB	All Points Bulletin.
APT	Asset Protection Team
APU	Auxiliary Power Unit-Electrical generator that supplies power and heat.
ATL	Attempt to Locate.
BlackStar	Anti-terrorist device carried on all US aircraft and vessels that carry nuclear weapons.
BOLO	Be on the lookout.
BSOG	BlackStar Operations Group – A strike force within the NSA that protects the BlackStar system.
DF	Direction Finder-equipment for tracing a radio signal.
GSW	Gunshot Wound.

IDACs	Indiana Data and Communication System
NCIC	National Crime Information Center
NDA	Non-Disclosure Agreement
NSA	National Security Agency - Conducts electronic surveillance programs and cryptologic support for US government agencies.
NSC	National Security Council - Advises the President and Congress.
NRO	National Reconnaissance Office - Responsible for surveillance satellite operation and data analysis.
PI	Philippine Islands
Signal 27	Initiating a traffic stop.
SITREP	Situation Report
SORT	Special Operations Response Team
SRT	Special Response Team
SYSOP	System Standard Operating Procedures

Suppressor Mechanical device used to reduce muzzle blast. Sometimes erroneously referred to as a silencer.

VIN Vehicle Identification Number

blackstar dc

Chapter 1

Suburban Chicago Hotel

Jake Thomas watched as two of Gregori Yancy's henchmen dragged a bound and gagged, semi-conscious Joanna Davies across the warehouse floor. Recovery of stolen nuclear weapons was the main objective but rescuing her was personal. They had pledged themselves to each other, and he would let nothing get in the way.

Her hazy eyes went wide when she saw Jake. She tried to say something, but one of the mercenaries hit her in the stomach with the butt of his weapon.

"No," Jake screamed involuntarily. Four other mercenaries heard and moved between him and Joanna. He pulled an M19111A from a snug position in a shoulder holster under his arm, aimed at a mercenary, and tried to pull the trigger.

Nothing happened. A second attempt brought no result, either.

Jake had heard of other operatives experiencing similar problems, but this was his first time. His trigger finger simply would not work.

Yancy's men pushed Joanna through a steel door and slammed it shut behind them. Jake moved toward the door but was blocked by the mercenaries as they formed a wall between him and Joanna.

One of them noted the problem Jake had with his weapon and leered as he moved in closer for the kill. He held an AK-47 mounted on a shoulder sling in front of him as he prepared to fire into Jake's midsection.

Jake stepped aside at the last moment and deflected the barrel away from him with his left hand. At the same time, he slid his right arm under the mercenary's left arm and planted a foot between the man's wide stance. He turned enough to draw the hapless thug up onto his back in a classic Judo move called Ogoshi, a hip throw.

Jake bent forward and effortlessly threw the man to the floor. He delivered a forefinger punch to the man's throat that crushed his windpipe,

Jake cleared his weapon and pulled the trigger. It bucked four times, and .45 caliber bullets struck the other three Russians.

One round shattered the shoulder of a bogey who pointed a Steyr machine pistol at him. The weapon clattered away on the concrete floor and leaned against the tire of a rented box van.

He did not try to retrieve it and raised his good hand as high as possible. "Do not shoot, for I surrender." His forehead blossomed with red spray a few seconds later as another mercenary shot him in the back of the head.

"Coward! We do not surrender to American pigs."

Jake fired two more rounds, which took the top of the shooter's head off. He watched as the man's body twitched and fell backward with vacant eyes locked onto rusty old pipes on the ceiling.

The incessant ringing of the cell phone jarred Jake Thomas awake. He fumbled around the walnut nightstand, knocked the phone off, found it, and answered the call with a grunt.

"Morning, Jake. Just wanted to make sure you're up and ready for our meeting in half an hour."

"Uncle Bob, is that you?" Jake answered in a slurred voice. *What happened to the other round? I know I hit another bad guy, even if it was only a dream.* He yawned and stretched as he continued, "Yeah, right, Bob. With only four hours sack time? I'll, um, uh, need to shave and shower. Meet you in the coffee shop in thirty."

"Sure thing. We need to finish up paperwork from yesterday and plan where we go from here."

"More? I can't think about paperwork until we rescue Joanna. I was up half the night working on reports."

"Just one perk of being the boss, and last time I checked, you still are. Should I order breakfast for you?"

His alcohol-sickened stomach churned at the thought of food. "Guess I have no choice but to get up and keep going. I need to find her, even if it kills me. I'll decide about breakfast when I get down there. See you in a few." He forced his aching body to a sitting position and sat on the edge of the bed while he waited for his pounding head to settle down. The dizziness went away after a while, and he took a chance at standing.

"What the...." Jake exclaimed as he set his foot on the carpet, and something crunched. He hoped it wasn't broken glass from his one-person party last night. He switched on the bedside lamp and stared at M & M candies scattered in a random pattern. *Guess I'll pick these up. Wouldn't be right to leave for the maids. Not sure how I could get along without M&Ms, though. Part of my support system.*

Jake walked into the noisy coffee shop twenty-eight minutes later and saw Uncle Bob wave at him from a booth in the back. Tim Cripe, their communications technician, and Jay Johansen, a senior agent, sat across the table from Bob. The smell of fried foods and burned toast wafted up from tables as he passed by and made him queasy. He exchanged nods with everyone at Bob's table and sat down next to him. A stout, middle-aged woman with dishwater-blonde hair plopped a cup in front of Jake and poured steaming hot coffee to the brim with a practiced flourish. She raised her voice to be heard above the surrounding chatter. "Name's Shirley. What can I get you, sir, or do you need a minute?"

"No, just an order of wheat toast for now, with a handful of those little packs of jelly, please. Doesn't matter what flavor." He reached for a square plastic container stuffed with sugar packets, tore four of them open, and poured them into his cup. The aroma of the coffee hit him as he stirred, and nausea returned. He concentrated on speaking to make it go away. "Nectar of the gods, especially on a morning like this. Okay, group, I don't know what I missed yesterday. The plan seemed airtight, given the intel we had, so what went wrong?"

The two men across from him sat quietly with hands folded on the table and offered only blank expressions in reply.

Uncle Bob cleared his throat. "Let's face it, Boss, you can plan a raid down to the smallest detail, but sometimes it just doesn't turn out the way you expected. Too many variables. It's the nature of our business."

"I know, and maybe I ask too much, but I wanted all of our top priority items checked off in one fell swoop."

"Which is what we were all shooting for. It just didn't happen for some reason. It will eventually come out in the wash."

"Unless the wash vaporizes us. I don't have to say how important our mission is, do I? We put a huge dent in Yancy's operation, but we didn't demolish it, and he still has Joanna. I can't lose her. I will not lose her. We need answers ASAP, so what will it take to get them?"

Bob waited while their server set the order of toast in front of Jake.

"Can I get you guys anything else?"

"No thanks, we're fine," Bob replied. He waited until she left to address the group, "Yancy will either go into deep hiding or make a break for it."

Jake offered a stony stare. "There's no way to guess which it will be, and this is no time for guessing. We need solid intel."

"Can't disagree with you on that, Boss. Problem is, we don't have real-time

8

intel we can count on, only gut feelings based on our combined experience."

"Yes, Bob, and those gut feelings have carried us a long way since the thefts at Mather. But, despite our best efforts, Yancy hasn't let any grass grow under his feet, and everything so far says he's headed east. Which means he has several routes open to him, including the Great Lakes. They used to call them the pre-industrial superhighway when water was the fastest way to move cargo."

"It would take the better part of a week to get to New York over the water."

"Yes, but he could travel almost undetected all the way. It boils down to how fast he wants to get wherever he's going. It may come down to a choice for him between getting there fast or staying concealed. He may also figure the longer it takes, the more we'll slack off. He didn't exactly waste time getting to Chicago but may decide to slow things down to throw us off."

Uncle Bob took a sip of lukewarm coffee and looked around for Shirley to get a warm-up. "You can drive yourself crazy thinking what a bad guy might do. On the other hand, since we don't have enough intel to go on, let's concentrate on what has happened up until now. It may show a pattern as to how he thinks and what he might do."

"You come up with any?"

"Sort of. Start by doing the math. Yancy used one device in Las Vegas and another in Deer Trail. We captured the other two in yesterday's raid, so it's down to the Black Star System, Agent Davies, and the remaining bad guys."

Jake stopped spreading blackberry jam on a piece of toast and looked up at Bob. "You were right up until a few minutes before I walked into the coffee shop."

"Okay, I'll bite. What happened between your room and here?"

Abandoned Food Service Warehouse in Lombard, Illinois

Joanna Davies sat with her back against the dingy wall of the dimly lit enclosure and mumbled, "I can't wait for Jake to rescue me. I have to find a way to escape, even if there's nothing here to help."

The locking mechanism of the heavy old door produced a hollow thunk as it unlocked. The metal-clad door swung open and brought a whoosh of fresh air. It was a welcome change from the ammonia-scented stale air of the old industrial walk-in freezer.

"Come with us, woman," commanded one of two men standing in the door. Bright light behind them hid their identity, but she could see a third figure behind them.

"Why?"

"You go to new place. No tricks, no problems, and we do not hurt you. Stay calm, and you live. *Понимаю*, uh, you understand, yes?"

"Yeah, I get it. Besides, how could I overcome three big, strong men?"

The third figure sneered. "You fight like tiger when we bring you to this place, so we take no chances. Is also order from our *Bocc*. We will handcuff and blindfold you to prevent escape. But you will die if you try."

Joanna lowered her eyes for a moment before replying. "I understand. Where are we going?"

"Disneyland, where else?" The third man laughed at his weak try at comedy. One of the other men followed his lead by chuckling.

"Destination is no concern for you, but is far, so use bucket as toilet."

"Not while you watch. Please close the door for a minute."

"Where can she go?" one of the men asked. He pulled the heavy door toward him, and the lock snapped shut.

She knocked on the door a moment later, and one of the men cautiously opened it. Joanna dumped the contents of the bucket on his head and tried to muscle past him.

He gasped in shock as he rubbed human waste off his face with his shirtsleeves. "I will kill you," he exclaimed as he blindly grabbed her arm with a steel grip.

Hotel Coffee Shop

Jake surveyed the men around the table in the noisy hotel coffee shop and lowered his voice, "I got an encrypted call from the Director on my way down here. It appears Yancy got more from the Alert Pad at Mather than we thought."

Uncle Bob's eyebrows went up. "Okay, maybe my math is off, but I thought they stole four devices and the BlackStar system from the bomber."

Jake leaned over within a few inches of Uncle Bob's ear. "As it turns out, there were six nukes," Jake said in a barely audible whisper.

"What the? How many...." Uncle Bob stopped short of saying the word out loud.

"Two bombs were left in a temporary shelter on the Alert Pad that was supposed to be used only during daylight hours. A weapons tech was running late for his daughter's softball game. Didn't want to take the time to return them to the Weapons Storage Area. Said he figured it was only overnight, and besides, they were locked in the Alert Pad, one of the most secure places on base."

Bob whistled. "Guess he found out how wrong that was. Bet some heads roll on that one."

"The weapons tech and his supervisor are facing courts-martial. However, higher-ups may decide disclosing security deficiencies would be a bad idea. Instead, they could transfer them to some garden-spot like Thule, Greenland, or Minot, North Dakota for the rest of their shortened careers. Either way, it looks like we're chasing two more devices than we thought. Which means we need to rethink Yancy's plan and double-down on our efforts."

A team member on the other side of the table had a puzzled look. "My ears are still ringing from the flash bangs we used yesterday, so I can only hear part of what you're saying. But I can tell by your expression it's probably not good news. What's going on?"

"I'll fill you in later," Jake answered.

Uncle Bob pulled a cellphone out of his pocket and flipped it open. "Yes, sir, hold on a minute." He put his hand over the phone and whispered to Jake, "I need to take this...be right back."

Unknown Warehouse Location in Elmhurst, Illinois

Gregori Yancy pounded his fists so hard on the heavy conference table it bounced off the carpeted floor. "Infernal agents of US Government raid other location. I lose men and equipment. Is good thing I am here. Is also unfortunate for them they chase their tails while I escape. Still, I ask, how do they know location?"

He paced around the tiny conference room, turned and said to his new right-hand man, "Vasily, you will supervise loading of trucks so we may soon leave this place. This is something Nestor would do, but unfortunately he is dead." *Of that I made sure.*

"Thank you for opportunity to lead men, *Bocc.* I will do good job for you."

"Good. Is no secret I need new lieutenant. You may be such if I can trust you."

"I will serve you with my life."

"Very good but let us hope it does not come to that," Yancy said with a wry smile. "I must think fast. US agents will not stop until I am dead or captured. Get road map so

I may know how to get to this Toledo, Ohio."

"*Bocc*, maybe is good idea to hide here…."

Yancy scowled and replied, "Do you not understand I wish to be away from here?"

"How soon do we go?"

"Yesterday is good, but I will accept two hours."

"*Da, Bocc.*

***

Chapter 2

Rural Virginia Lakeside Property

"The idiots the Consortium sends me," Jack Morgan exclaimed as he launched an empty Jack Daniels bottle like a baseball pitch at the log wall of the cabin. It shattered into hundreds of pieces that scattered across the floor. The afternoon sun turned them into prisms and splashed a rainbow of colors around the living room. "Half-trained and incompetent. It's enough to drive a man crazy. Know what I mean?"

"Wild" Bill Johnson, his middle-aged bodyguard, sat in an Adirondack-style lounge chair. He picked lint off a black knit sweater stretched across his ample midsection. Outbursts like this were common, so Bill waited patiently for his boss to continue. He spoke up after an awkward silence, "Don't know, boss. Seems like the devil himself is throwing roadblocks at you."

"I don't believe in the Devil, but if there was one, I'd be his main competition. Right now, I'm trying to decide which way to go."

"I ain't the least bit worried, Boss. You'll come up with something. You always do. I mean, Winfield may not be dead, but he's out of the picture, and that's half the battle, ain't it?"

Morgan let loose an expressive sigh. "True, but I never ever settle for half, now do I?"

"You don't, and I got faith in you. You always do, and this time ain't gonna be no different."

"Thanks, Bill. That makes me feel better. Must be why I keep you around. That and the good coffee you make." Morgan smiled. "But back to business. I need to find

Winfield real soon. They moved him to another safehouse after the last attack."

"Sure would make it easier if Justin Todd still worked in the Director's office. How's old Justin doing, anyway? Haven't heard much about him lately," Bill said hesitantly.

"I've got a line on him. I'll have him stashed in one of my safehouses before tomorrow night."

"I figure you wrapped him up a long time ago and dumped in a lake where he won't never be found."

"You see why I'm the boss? I have a longer view than most people. Justin might prove useful, especially where the Consortium comes in."

"He worked for them, didn't he?"

"Yes, and I may need to remind them at some point. First, though, I've got to get the Feds off my back. Justin may come in handy for that."

A puzzled look crossed Bill's face. "How so, Boss?"

"I'm not ready to say. Back to Winfield. I know they're hiding him somewhere in DC, and we're getting close. I have two of my best guys working on pinning down his exact location. They will come up with something soon or lose a fat bonus. One thing you can be sure of, Bart Winfield is a dead man. In the meantime, we need to fly to Chicago."

"Why Chicago, Boss?"

"You should know better than to ask. Call the hangar. Tell them to top off the jet and file a flight plan to Chicago. Tell them to rent a full-sized Suburban this time."

Abandoned Food Service Warehouse

Yevgeny's partner stood stock still at the sight of his comrade covered in excrement.

Their leader pointed an H&K MP-5 9mm machine pistol at Joanna and said in a low growl, "Listen, or you die. Lay down on stomach. Put arms behind back and do not move."

The underling who was not busy wiping his face drew a blue steel Smith & Wesson Model 559, 9mm pistol from a Bianchi shoulder rig and pointed it at her face.

Joanna could usually rely on her extensive training to take out both, but she knew her weakened condition lowered the odds considerably. She slowly dropped to the floor and waited like a caged animal.

Yvgeny finished wiping his face and dropped to his knees next to her with the smell of an outhouse clinging to him. He soon had her subdued with handcuffs and ankle restraints. He flipped her over, unsnapped her pants, and pulled down the zipper.

"No," Joanna whimpered.

"What is this you do, Yvgeny?"

"Shut up, Igor. Is no concern to you."

"*Nyet*, we are team. We will also pay if you anger *Bocc*. He says do not hurt her."

"Hurt her? She will smile when I finish."

The leader stepped forward and waved his weapon. "Do not do this now. There will be time later to pleasure her and you."

Yvgeny leaned close to Joanna's ear and whispered, "You will feel my full force later, and beg me to continue. For now, you will smell crap all the way to where we go." He wiped the soiled cloth across her face and rubbed it all over her head. "Turn head away."

"No, please do not gag me," she said through clenched teeth.

"Choice is not yours. We take no chance this time. You will have gag."

"I promise I won't scream, but I don't want… to… be gagged."

"What you want is no concern."

He tied the gag tightly around her nose and mouth as she fought to breathe. The thick fabric of the hood limited air even more.

She concentrated on the rescue that must be in the works. *I must keep faith. Hope is all I have.*

"Put her in cargo space of truck near front corner," the leader ordered. "Guard her with your very lives."

The two guards shoved Joanna to the wood-plank floor of a nondescript rental truck a few minutes later that left a splinter in her leg. She screamed in pain, but the gag and hood muffled the sound. The back door of the truck slammed shut with a dull thud as a lock slid closed.

Joanna thought about the actions she took before they dragged her out of the freezer. Any forensic crew would find the half-dozen clues she left behind.

The scribbled BSOG-JD on the dingy white freezer walls she did in urine would stand out like a sore thumb. It would be almost invisible to the naked eye but would show up like a neon sign under a blacklight, especially when sprayed with luminol.

She spat on the walls and ceiling until her mouth was dry and cut herself on a nail to spread drops of blood around. There were plenty of DNA samples in the enclosed area.

"How long does trip take?" one guard asked the other.

The other guard scowled. "Does not matter. Say nothing of consequence in front of girl."

"I do not understand why we must bring her with us. I would shoot her and dump body in ditch."

"I think Yancy wants her boyfriend to follow us."

"Why would he do such a thing? Is better to be away from agents who pursue us, especially boyfriend. He will not stop."

"*Bocc* has personal reason to lure him. Sasha says reason is death of brother of *Bocc*. We must follow orders, for I do not wish to die by *Bocc's* hand. You should think this way also."

"True, but I am bored. I must have something to amuse me."

"Well, there is girl…."

"I do not wish to die any more than you. Do you want to play *Durak?*"

"I have heard of this card game, but do not know how to play."

"I will show you," Yvgeny said as he pulled a deck of thirty-six cards from his pocket.

Hotel Lobby

Uncle Bob settled into a secluded seating area a few minutes later. "Sorry, Director, it was a little too noisy in the coffee shop."

"Sounded like it," John Banner, the director of the National Security Agency replied. "Jake isn't with you, is he?"

"No, sir, he's still in the coffee shop. What can I do for you?"

"I'm not sure where to begin. You are still close to Jake, aren't you?"

"You could say that. More than anybody else on the team. Is there a problem?"

"I don't know. That is why I'm calling you, and not him. The failure in Chicago has a lot of people on edge. What is your assessment?"

"I wouldn't call it a complete failure. Maybe you should be talking to Jake. After all, he's...."

"But I'm not. You are the most senior agent under him, so I want your opinion. Can he handle the job, given the kidnapping of Davies? I don't know many men who could stay focused, given his relationship to her."

"I'm not quite sure what you mean, Director."

"Don't be coy with me, Bob. I know they have been seeing each other, and it might be turning serious. I need to know if he can handle the pressure. You have known Jake longer than anybody in the agency. Did you work with him on a recovery op in the Philippines years ago?"

"I did. He was still in the Air Force and helped recover classified equipment from a crash site. Worked with our team like he'd been doing it all his life. In fact, I recommended him for a position with us."

"Which has worked out very well. His work has been outstanding, which is why I chose him to be team chief when I moved Bart Winfield into the Deputy Director position after you turned me down."

"Didn't want to be Deputy Director, or Team Chief, for that matter. Too many politics, and too much paperwork."

"I understand and have never held it against you. On the other hand, even though you are close to Jake, I need an honest opinion. Can he handle the pressure or not? I don't want to remove him as team chief, even temporarily. It would kill his career."

"More than likely, sir, and the NSA is his life. Only Joanna is more important."

"That's what I thought, so I won't take any action, at least for now. What I would like you to do is be my eyes and ears…."

"You want me to spy on him?"

"Not exactly, but I'm sure you understand my situation. This is one of the most important investigations we have conducted since the Cold War. Actually, now that I think about it, the most important since World War II. I need to know what is happening, and short of flying there myself, you are my best option."

"I'm flattered, and yes, I'll keep an eye on things. What should I do if things go south?"

"I will put a letter in my desk that explains the situation and makes you Co-Team Chief. I'll tear it up if everything goes well. But if it does not, you can step in with the authority to act. I hope it doesn't become necessary."

"Same here, Director."

"Well, since we understand each other, I'll let you get back to work."

Uncle Bob ended the call and thought of the night before. He was headed back to his room from the hotel bar well after midnight when he noticed the door to Jake's room was slightly ajar. There was no obvious damage from being kicked open, but it was something an agent could not ignore. "Jake, you okay?" Bob slowly entered the room with his hand resting on the Glock-17 service pistol in a side holster. "You okay, Boss?"

Two more steps revealed Jake curled up on the floor on the other side of the bed with an empty whiskey bottle beside him. Bob gently nudged the prone figure, who had begun to snore. "Better get you to bed, brother." *More like the son I lost in Vietnam.*

He checked Jakes' pulse and put a hand in front of the younger man's nose to make sure he was breathing. He carefully hoisted the limp body and struggled to get him onto the bed a few feet away. "Man, you reek of whiskey."

Jake stirred but did not awaken.

Bob checked the rest of the room to make sure everything else was in order. "Let's get your shoes off and loosen that belt," he mumbled. "And while I'm at it, guess I should pull the blanket up over you. Man, I hate to see you like this."

He locked the door behind him and tiptoed away on the plush hallway carpet.

Storage Facility, Beltsville, Maryland

"Wake up, Justin Todd, or Glenn Marks, or whatever your real name is," Jack Morgan said as he leaned over the man lying on a couch in a luxury RV. "Although, I think I prefer to call you Justin, the name you used when you worked in the NSA Director's office. Do you have any idea how hard it was to find you? And yet, I did."

Justin heard the words through a hazy blur of pain and dizziness. He tried to sit up, but restraints on his hands and ankles left him helpless. He moved his head from side to side, which brought on even more pain.

"Yes, you're still in your RV in the storage facility. That's how I tracked you down. I knew you were too smart to fly out of anywhere on the East Coast. Your former coworkers would have nailed you in an instant. Staying in hotels would let them track you, even if you paid in cash. So, an RV was the best option. See, it pays to think like a criminal. My men are going through this palace on wheels a foot at a time. You did a good job of planning your escape. Too bad I was one step ahead of you."

Justin tried to speak, but the wound around his throat from a garrote was painfully inflamed. He could not produce more than a gurgle, and it was difficult to breathe. Justin finally gave up and let his head fall back.

***

Chapter 3

Warehouse in Elmhurst Illinois

"Bocc, last cargo truck has arrived," Vasily called out to Yancy.

"Good. Trucks are fueled and ready?"

"Of this, I am sure."

"Gather men, so I may give them orders. We leave five minutes after."

Yancy addressed the assembled men ten minutes later, "Vasily will drive SUV and two trucks. I will take other SUV. Rental truck follows in last position. We go by different routes when we leave warehouse and meet on highway. Each driver must know where to go and what to do if police stop them. Take no chances with my cargo."

"Yes, *Bocc.*"

"Do not draw attention to you. If police stop you, take no action without my permission. Do not shoot unless I shoot first...."

A murmur arose from the group.

"Do you question me?" Yancy asked a tall man with wavy blond hair.

"Never, *Bocc,* but I am trained to shoot first."

"In other countries that would be good, but not here. Do what police say within reason. But first you must tell me by radio you are detained. I will free you. Of this you can be sure."

"*Da, Bocc.*"

"Do not bunch together. Go to different petrol stations for fuel but stay close. One man stays with vehicle all the time. We leave in five minutes. Do you understand instructions?"

The question was met with a chorus of yes and *da*. The blond-haired man shrugged his shoulders and commented, "We are professional. This will be easy."

Yancy shrugged his shoulders. "Maybe…maybe not. This time we are chased by professionals. Be vigilant."

"Da, Bocc."

Storage Facility, Beltsville, Maryland

Jack Morgan watched as Justin Todd's head fell back on the pillow. "Good idea. Sit back and relax while I do all the talking. You may recognize me since I attended several meetings in your old boss's office. I'm Jack Morgan."

Justin's eyes widened as he remembered Morgan and tried to scoot away.

"Settle down, my friend. I'm not here to harm you. In fact, my men saved you from the hit man who put that nasty wound around your neck. Actually, I'm here to help. Our mutual friends at the Consortium targeted you for 'Extreme Sanction.' In other words, they sent the assassin who tried to kill you. I saved you, and now here we are. Listen to what I have to offer, and we might end up being lifelong friends, not like the loser who tried to kill you."

Wild Bill glanced back at a lifeless body lying in the narrow aisle behind him.

Morgan grimaced. "You were losing your value as an asset to the Consortium, especially when they felt you compromised yourself through negligence. You are in quite a pickle, Justin. The NSA suspects you of being a mole, and the Consortium fears you jeopardized the operation. They had to kill two NSA agents to protect your identity. As you can imagine, that did not sit well with them. Furthermore, I would think whoever was in your apartment probably didn't have your best interests in mind either."

Justin closed his eyes, shrugged, and slowly nodded.

Morgan continued, "Let's start with how I can help you recover from the predicament you got yourself into. For a start, I have friends in high places who can return you to the NSA by snapping their fingers. Nobody will suspect you work for me."

Morgan walked to the refrigerator and pulled out a Diet Coke. "Who drinks this diet stuff, anyway? Tastes like a chemical plant. You want anything, while I'm up?"

Justin shook his head.

"Suit yourself." Morgan sat in a chair across from the couch. "I have a doctor coming to patch up the nasty effects of the garrote. It will serve as proof of your kidnapping and torture. You managed to escape and will be found drugged and wandering the street near your old apartment. Trust me, this will work," Morgan said with a grin.

"You seem to have devised a foolproof plan," Justin said. "Besides, what choice do I have?"

"Well, it's true, your choices are seriously limited. So, rest and enjoy the peace. The guards are here to protect you from attempts by the Consortium to terminate your employment and your life. We'll move you to a more suitable location that fits the escape scenario tomorrow."

Morgan paused before continuing, "On to my second point. I need information about the whereabouts of the Winfields. Don't shake your head. You may not know their exact location, but you know various safehouses where the Assistant Director of the NSA and his agent wife might be staying. He may be in a coma, but I still need to find him, and you will help me."

Justin grimaced, hung his head, and said nothing.

NSA Safehouse, Ellicott City, Maryland

Nora Winfield pressed the receive button on the satellite phone, "Hello, Director."

"How did you know it was me?"

"Who else besides Jake would call on a satellite phone this late at night?"

"Always on top of things, as usual. It seems I can never get ahead of you."

"That's why you pay me the big bucks. I do love talking to you, John, but I'm guessing you didn't call to chit-chat."

"No, unfortunately not. I have been told that somebody is quietly looking for Bart, and I'm guessing it's not because they need a fourth partner for bridge."

"Not too quiet, apparently, since you heard about it."

"It's why I get paid the big bucks. You hear things when you hold your ear to the ground long enough. I made some inquiries, and it seems Jack Morgan may have been behind the attack that injured Bart. Intel is still a bit sketchy, but I'm afraid he may take another run at Bart and you. I'm going to send a couple more guards per shift to keep you two safe. You will have two inside the building and two on the grounds. Jerome Scoggins will supervise and act as a roving guard. I'm afraid I can't free any more assets until I get confirmation of an actual attack."

"Thanks, John. Morgan has a vendetta that goes back to when Bart broke up the smuggling operation in Seawind Bay."

"I'll continue to investigate him and hope something turns up. Unfortunately, I'm a little shorthanded...."

"I know, and I have to admit, I'm torn. I could be helpful there in the office tracking down leads. On the other hand, no one can protect Bart better than me."

"Can't disagree with that."

"Once we've cleared the threat from Morgan, I think I might like to come back to work, even if it's only a few hours a day. What do you think?"

"You're one of the very few people I trust without hesitation. Yes, I would love to have you in the office, even for a few hours a day. Set your own schedule, and I will assign extra guards to Bart when you are here."

"Thank you for your generosity, John. I'll be forever indebted to you."

"Don't mention it. I'm glad we can help each other. Sorry, but I need to run. I have a Congressional Intelligence Sub-Committee meeting in twenty minutes, and it's a ten-minute walk. But let's stay in touch."

"Absolutely." Nora ended the call and said to her comatose husband, "You and John are the only people in this business I trust one hundred percent."

I-94, Eastbound from Chicago

"Looks like our hunch was right," Jake said to Uncle Bob. "Satellite scans show multiple radios on frequencies we think the suspects are using left Chicago heading east."

"As my grandma used to say, 'Even a blind sow gets lucky now and then,'" Bob replied.

Jake turned from gazing out the passenger window at distant flashes of lightning from the thunderstorm that had moved south. "By the way, thanks for throwing out that half-eaten fish sandwich. Really stunk up the truck."

Uncle Bob took his right hand off the wheel long enough to wag a finger at Jake. "And thank you for throwing out your three cups of stale coffee that smelled like old farts. It was not making for good ambiance."

"Ambiance? What, are you reading literary novels again?"

"A man's got to stay grounded."

"Probably a good idea. Ouch, and speaking of grounded, my butt went to sleep again. These cross-country chases sure take a toll on the body."

"Not like getting shot, but yeah, they sure do. I'll be glad when Yancy and crew are behind bars, and I can keep my feet on the ground for a while."

"Me, too," Jake replied. "Yech."

"What, is that gum a little stale?"

"No doubt about it. Last time I chew a piece from the back of the glove compartment. You remember Bosnia?"

"Five years ago? Although it feels like yesterday. Won't forget it anytime soon, even if I try. Why bring it up now?"

"Director reminded me earlier how we tracked bad guys back then by using their radio frequencies."

Bob smiled. "Like we're doing now?"

"Which proves my point. Nothing ever changes, does it? Same methods, just different places, and actors."

"Ain't that the truth. Think how Bosnia could have turned out. You crawled into the bottle then…."

"I, uh…."

"Sorry, I didn't mean to throw it up to you. And before you get all defensive on me, you don't have to make excuses. I know Joanna being taken is a horrible monkey on your back. But I'm telling you right here and now, the bottle won't help."

"No, but it helps numb my mind."

"I understand that. You'll snap out of it before long, and you know I have your six as long as I'm alive and kicking."

"I count on it, and likewise."

They sat in silence until the radio sparked to life and startled them. "BSOG-1, this is Comm-1."

"Comm-1, go for BSOG-1."

"I'm picking up an encrypted signal on the right frequency. Problem is the private line tone is locking out our differentiating equipment. Direction finder is locked on, but I can't triangulate their exact position without two more positions."

"At least we know the approximate direction they're heading. What else you got?"

"Signal strength is a level three ninety degrees, which means we're within fifty miles or so. Picking up four, no, make that five different signals. Means there's at least that many vehicles."

"If two people had radios in the same truck, would that show as one or two hits?"

"One. It would be two only if both radios were transmitting at the same time. Not likely to happen. Two men in a truck would probably share one radio. Straight ahead fifty miles gives us a good jump on them. It's just a matter of time."

"Good. I like the way you think."

"Thanks. You know we're gonna get her back, right?"

"Thanks, I appreciate that."

Jake stared straight ahead into the darkness.

Ten Minutes Later

"BSOG-1, this is Comm-1."

"Go for BSOG-1."

"Signal strength is still hovering at a three, but the position has changed. DF shows it at a 160-degree angle instead of ninety, and the dial shows it's dropped to a Level two. Must have turned off onto I-80."

"Let me check the atlas for the next exit to I-80 while you recheck your data."

"Checking…yup, I'm sure. DF meter shows 165 degrees magnetic, and the strength dropped to a level 2."

"Fifteen miles to State Road 249, Bob. It's a shortcut to I-80."

"Aye, aye, Boss."

"All units, this is BSOG-1. Take the State Road 249 exit south to I-80, the Indiana Toll Road. Let me know if it changes."

"Will do, Boss."

T.c. Miller and J.A. Schrock

***

Chapter 4

Indiana Toll Road Near Elkhart, Indiana

"Holy cow, can you imagine that. Running across Trooper Terry Taets. Guess I'll just have to make a little house call."

Trooper Bill Hubbard smiled as he turned into the median and pulled up next to another marked Indiana State Police unit parked in the opposite direction. "Look who's poaching my game today."

"Proud to do my duty, hotshot. By the way, just because you pulled up next to me doesn't mean I have to share what I catch."

"True, TT, unless I get to them first," Bill replied as they sat driver's-door-to-driver's door. "So, how many years you got on the job?"

TT cupped his chin in his hand and stared at the headliner. "Let me see now, just over thirty-one years. Nine months makes it an even 32, and I'm gonna pull the pin to max out my pension. After that, I'm gone fishing. You coming to the picnic the wife and me are having this weekend?"

"Planning on it. In fact, I think Bonnie's looking forward to it more than me."

"Always good when the wife is on board. Hopefully, this rain will stop by then. Although, truth be told, I love the smell of pavement after a good downpour."

"Me, too. 'Course, I'd like it a whole lot better if we didn't have to do traffic stops. Getting all wet and having to clean your weapon when you get home to avoid rust is no picnic. Remember what they said in the academy, 'Your weapon is your life.'"

TT laughed, "One of the few things they said that made any sense."

"Ain't that the truth. Geez, look at that line of trucks headed this way. Four or five hanging tight. Gotta be some kind of violation in there."

"They're on your side, but I'll take anything either one of us sees. Doesn't look like the lead truck is speeding, and Lord knows I don't want the extra paperwork."

"This shift is dragging on, isn't it? Feels like it's never going to…."

"Whoa there, Nelly. The last truck doesn't have any lights on the rear, so tag along if you want."

Hubbard activated the light bar on top of the cruiser as he rapidly accelerated. He watched as the line of trucks slowed for a moment before regaining speed. The target vehicle slowly pulled to the shoulder. "Dispatch, 24-130, signal-27."

"Go ahead, 24-130 for your traffic stop."

"Got a yellow Ryder rental, Colorado truck plate AUX-989, I-80 east of State Road 19 exit. Need you to run it."

"Roger, 24-130."

Hubbard brought the cruiser to a stop ten feet behind the rental truck. He left his emergency lights flashing and stepped out into the cool night air, as he adjusted his hat and duty belt. He walked cautiously toward the driver's side of the stopped Ryder truck as his eyes adjusted to the flashing red and blue lights reflected off the pull-down door on the back. The cruiser's lights were the only illumination in the area, other than the occasional vehicle whizzing by.

The experienced trooper noted a commercial-grade padlock on the rear door and looked underneath to make sure nobody was trying to sneak up on him from the passenger side. Bill unsnapped his holster as he walked up behind the driver's door. "Morning, Trooper Hubbard, Indiana State Police. Do you know you have no lights on the rear of your truck?"

"No, officer, this I did not know."

"We will soon fix," said a figure in the passenger seat.

"No problem, gentlemen, but I need to see your license, registration, and rental paperwork, and please turn on the dome light so I can see you, please."

Hubbard noticed Taets had pulled up behind his unit. He turned back to the driver. "Like I said, paperwork, please."

"Of course, officer. Here is license."

"I also need your vehicle registration and lease paperwork."

"Is not to be found."

"I think I'd start in the glove box if I were you. Anything in there I need to be aware of, like weapons, drugs, or atomic bombs?"

"No, Officer. I tell you the truth."

Neither occupant reacted to my weak attempt at humor. "Hey, T, can you cover the passenger door?"

Taets moved out from behind the headlights of Hubbard's cruiser. It was a simple but effective technique that allowed him to remain hidden in darkness until needed. He moved toward the passenger door and used the oversized side mirror to observe the two occupants.

BSOG Command Vehicle

Jake answered the call from John Banner. "Hey, Boss, how are things in DC?"

"Same mixture of deception and intrigue, and that's just on the congressional front. The other side of the coin is more unpredictable. I have more information...."

"About Agent Davies?"

"No, wish I did. It's about Yancy and crew. New satellite intel says they're on frequencies used mostly by the Russians."

"Are they still on I-80?"

"Indeed, they are. Last satellite pass showed Yancy's gang east of you."

"Then we'll more than likely catch up to them soon, sir."

"I have all the confidence in the world in you. You are doing stellar work. In fact, I would say on the same level as Bart and Nora. I knew you would be the right man to lead the field team."

"Thank you, sir. How is Bart?"

"Not much change in the last week or two. Doctors want to keep him in a coma to help him heal. Nora's keeping watch over him. As the cliché goes, time will tell. I only wish he were back in the Executive Suite.

"You and me both. Uh, not to cut it short, but I should get back to chasing Yancy."

"Agreed, but one last thing before I go. I have a report that Jack Morgan may be headed your way."

"I wondered when that turncoat would pop up again. Any idea when or where he might rear his ugly head?"

"No idea at this point, but I'll let you know as soon as I find out. For the time being, watch your six."

"Will do, sir. But that's why I have Uncle Bob."

Indiana Toll Road

"The fact that you don't have papers on the rental makes me wonder if maybe it's stolen," Hubbard said to the driver. "Both of you need to step out of the truck and move to the rear. There, now put both hands on the rear door and spread your feet."

The men said nothing and complied.

"Well, look at what we have here," Hubbard said as he tucked a semi-automatic pistol into the back of his duty belt. You best have a carry permit for this pistol, pal, or we have a problem. He continued the search and removed a six-inch stiletto knife from the man's boot, as well as a box knife from his back pocket.

Taets stood off to the side with a hand on the butt of his duty weapon.

"Gonna handcuff you, so don't get frisky," Hubbard said. He placed the driver's arms behind his back and cuffed him. "I'm going to sit you down on the bumper and want you to cross your legs. Hey, watch out, T, we got a runner."

The other suspect spun around and got one foot down before TT's foot slid in front and tripped him. He drove his shoulder into the man's back with enough force to knock him over the knee-high metal barricade at the edge of the shoulder.

The hapless suspect tumbled onto the grass on the other side with a dazed look of surprise.

Taets quickly holstered his weapon, stepped over the barricade, and pinned the man to the ground with a knee in his back. He grabbed a set of handcuffs from his duty belt, hooked the man up, and patted him down. "Well, now," TT said with a grin, "Looks like you've got a firearm, too. Don't suppose you have a permit for this, do you?"

The suspect squirmed and said nothing.

The trooper helped the man over the vehicle barricade and sat him on the truck bumper next to the driver.

Hubbard stood in front of them in a wide stance with hands-on-hips. "I'll ask both of you, do you have a permit to carry?"

Both men sat still and stared straight ahead. One looked at the other and started to speak but stopped when his partner shot an icy look at him.

"Keep an eye on them, TT, while I search the cab of the truck and get the VIN."

Hubbard walked toward the front of the truck and exclaimed a minute later, "What the hell?"

"What you got there, Bill?"

"Enough weapons and ammo to take on the entire Toll Road Post. Furthermore, that damn SUV is still sitting up there watching us."

"Dispatch, this is 24-130."

"Go ahead, 24-130."

"Send a couple more units this way for backup. We have an arsenal here and a dark-colored SUV about a half-mile east that appears to be observing us."

"Copy that, 24-130."

"After that, let me know when you're ready to copy a VIN."

"Ready to copy, 24-130."

Hubbard read the VIN into the mike clipped to the epaulet on his uniform shirt while keeping a trained eye on the SUV.

"Twenty-Four-One-Thirty, subject VIN was reported stolen out of a rental lot in Deer Trail, Colorado two weeks ago."

"Roger, Dispatch. Send a wrecker to our location, and while you're at it, notify the First Sergeant we'll need a search warrant."

"Copy that, 24-130."

I-80 Eastbound, Indiana Toll Road

Bob turned toward Jake. "How far away did the director say they were?"

"Not far, and since they're showing up on the DF, I'm betting they're making a run toward the eastern seaboard."

"Well, we won't know anytime soon since the satellite covering this area only flies over every four hours."

"I'll call Banner and see if he can get another satellite repositioned."

"You can do that, even though we're kind of a secret squirrel thing?"

"We need a little help from above right now, and he can get us a satellite."

John Banner directed his assistant to make the arrangements for increased satellite surveillance, and returned to the call with Jake.

"While I have you on the phone, we need to discuss your two charges for a minute."

"Alicia and Star?" Jake asked. "They're at FE Warren with Gwen Harding. I thought it was safer to house them on a military base until we capture Yancy. Plus, they have the gyms to work out in."

"I agree. Gwen says their training is going well and gave them high marks. Apparently, though, Alicia told her she wants to visit her father's grave in Seawind Bay. Gwen also said Star's mother visited a few weeks ago before she started her worldwide concert tour."

"Yes, sir. I got involved in that visit. Star wanted to travel with Joan, but most of the venues are in foreign countries, so I advised against it. Security would be a logistical nightmare, even with help from Joan's private staff. Thankfully, Joan agreed. Gwen said it upset Star for a few days, but some hard training helped take her mind off the matter."

"It has come back up, and I want to handle it diplomatically. So, I would like to turn it over to you. Licia and Star look up to you and your team and follow your advice. I can arrange for a plane to fly you there if you want to talk to them in person."

"Whatever you think is best, sir. But I feel like I need to keep heading east. We may be only hours away from catching Yancy."

"It is your call as Team Leader, but would you persuade them to not visit Sea Wind Bay right away? They will listen to you. I am also glad you have been talking to Nora on a regular basis. She is tough as nails, but we have to understand what she is going through, and give her our support."

"Yes, sir. Bart and Nora are the closest thing to family I have. Nora says doctors are hopeful about Bart's recovery, but also said it'd be a long, hard road ahead."

"Yes, he has got to come out of the coma first, and faces up to a year of rest and recuperation. Sorry, but I need to go. By the way, recovering two of the devices showcased your management skills, and will reflect in my annual evaluation. Anyway, keep up the outstanding work, and let me know the second you have something solid."

"Roger that, sir."

St. Lawrence Seaway Onboard the Ocean-Going Vessel *SP Lee*

"Captain Gorsky, we're listing seven degrees to port," the helmsman shouted over howling wind and sheets of rain pounding against the wheelhouse windows. Waves crashed violently against the steel hull and rocked the ship from bow to stern.

"Steady into wind," Pavel Gorsky ordered. Although he had been through much worse during his thirty-four years on the sea, he kept a white-knuckled grip on the wall-mounted handrail. "Three degrees to starboard."

"Aye, aye, Captain, three degrees to starboard. Good, she's steadying out."

Gorsky turned to Andy McDonough, the First Mate. "From where, I ask, did this come? You did not post in morning briefing."

"Blew up from nowhere, sir. The Seaway is worse than I remember."

"No matter, ship will settle once we add to ballast tanks."

"Aye, Captain, although it's kind of nice having such a light load. Saves fuel and makes the manifest simple."

"Is true on both counts."

"Makes you wonder if the company is making any money on these trips." Andy saw Gorsky's eyebrows go up and almost regretted his comment. "What I, uh, mean is I plan to work for them until retirement. Just want to make sure they're on solid ground."

Gorsky smiled and Andy relaxed.

"Is good you keep company interests in mind but lose no sleep. Commissioners know this business of that you can be sure. We are specialized support ship for vital trips. Some cargo cannot be shipped by big lines. Too much chance for loss or damage. Our work is important to Consortium."

"I know, but I…."

Andy was interrupted by the inner door to the captain's cabin crashing against the steel bulkhead. A blonde-haired girl barely of school age laughed and giggled as she burst onto the bridge. "Papa, Mama is being too serious. You must make her laugh."

Pavel scooped the girl up in his arms and brushed curls from her glowing face. Her bright blue eyes seemed to light up the bridge. "Soon, my little Sugar Plum. But first, Papa has work, so you must return to cabin, please."

"Oh, Papa, now you are being too serious. No one wants to have fun."

"We all do, but we must also work." Pavel knelt, turned her around and pointed her to the door. "Now go," he said in a voice that was stern enough to propel her toward the cabin. "I will come for lunch. Cook says he has made my favorite borscht."

"Then borscht must also be my favorite. But Mama and I are hungry now," she replied with only the hint of a pout."

"Tell mama I will come in twenty minutes."

***

Chapter 5

Indiana Toll Road

Hubbard addressed the suspects as they sat on the ground next to the rental truck, "Since we can't figure out who you really are, and you have enough weapons and ammo to start a war, we're taking you to our Toll Road Post. Your truck will be impounded pending a search warrant. Unless, of course, you want to open the cargo door so we can have a look inside." He waited for a moment before continuing, "Didn't think so. Look, you have a lot of hard questions to answer when we get to the post. You can get the ball rolling by telling us what you're up to. Let's start with your names."

The suspects responded with sullen looks and watched as a tow truck driver hooked up the rental. They silently stared at the ground without answering, so the troopers loaded the men into separate cruisers and followed the tow truck as it headed east.

Hubbard watched for the mystery SUV but didn't notice it had pulled off at the next exit. The driver waited for the troopers and tow truck to pass before following at a discreet distance.

"Dispatch, 24-130. Twenty-Four Forty-Eight and I are en route to the Post behind the tow truck."

"Copy that 24-130."

Hubbard glanced in the rearview mirror through the cage partition. "What should I call you?" he asked his prisoner. "'Hey-you', just doesn't cut it."

The man avoided eye contact and stared out the rear passenger window into the faint light of the oncoming dawn.

Bill continued, "Love the smell of crisp air after a rain. Personally, I think dawn is the best part of the day. You know, all clean and new."

No response.

"Guess you're just not the talkative type. Your choice, but I think I'll call you Fred. It'll have to do until I know your real name."

The man stared back with a smirk.

"You do know you and your buddy are in a boat-load of trouble, don't you? Weapons charges, stolen truck, and that's just a start. Once a judge signs a search warrant, I bet we tack on more charges for whatever's in the back of the stolen rental."

Fred continued to ignore Trooper Hubbard and offered only a grunt in reply.

St. Lawrence Seaway Aboard the *SP Lee*

"Now, where we were?" Captain Gorsky asked Andy. "Oh, yes, cargo. As always, contents are no concern of ours. We load where told and deliver where orders say. We should have no problem if Mother Nature cooperates."

"Yes, Captain."

Pavel paused and a serious look crossed his face. "For how many voyages have you been my First Mate?"

"Thirty-seven over two-years, sir. I've lost track of how many times we have crossed the Atlantic together. It's not even our first time in the St Lawrence Seaway. And can't say I want to do it again very soon either, especially with weather like this. We're a little closed in for my comfort."

"I must agree. There was note in the morning report about difficulty with hatch?"

"Had some trouble with cargo hatch three, but finally got it battened down. Crew chief used a trick he learned in the academy from one of the salty instructors."

The helmsman sneezed twice and remarked, "Man, this damp air is killing my sinuses."

"Bless you," Andy replied. "And the fresh coat of paint we did in port didn't help either, did it?"

"I'll get over it. Look, a ray of sunshine peeking through the overcast."

"Is good sign," Captain Gorsky remarked as the steady hum of the engines sent low vibrations throughout the ship.

Consortium Headquarters, Leipzig, Switzerland

"You should not feel compelled to defend yourself, Mister Wilhelm. Even I might have been fooled by the message you received had I not checked with the issuing official to ensure its authenticity. Which, of course, is something you were not permitted to do."

The Commissioner stared at the file in his hands for a moment before he continued, "The position you held is of vital importance to our organization. I must admit the timing of your departure from the Deer Trail facility seemed suspicious, and entirely too coincidental. So, I examined a copy of the message you received, and I can see how you were deceived. The classified encoding appeared authentic, even to a trained eye."

Gunter stared silently. *This does not sound like the Commissioner I am used to. I would expect him to want my head on a platter.*

"Our technicians discovered a deeply hidden keystroke monitoring system in your computer that reported every action to an encrypted relay server in Albania. It was then transmitted to an untraceable location in North America. I suspect it eventually ended up in the hands of someone who does not have the best interest of the Consortium in mind. Therefore, I permanently terminated the employment of the security person who failed to block the intrusion and do not hold you responsible."

Gunter sighed with relief.

The Commissioner also relaxed and leaned back with a look of sadness and nostalgic resignation. "It would appear that an unknown entity has targeted our organization. I remember when only the major powers had intelligence services. Now, it seems every employee of a former Soviet Bloc country wants to strike out on their own. Most of them have become associates. Others have chosen to muddy international waters with a haphazard and chaotic approach to our profession. It is possible the person who targeted you is one Jack Morgan. You are familiar with him, yes?"

"I am indeed. He is a disgraced former agent of the US Drug Enforcement Agency."

"Yes, it seems he is running operations that conflict with our organizational goals."

"I started a dossier on him but could not develop a contact within his core cadre. He worked with former Soviet agents who ran a smuggling operation on the West coast of North America."

"What were they smuggling?"

"The usual drugs, weapons, and occasionally people. I was so focused on the acquisition of nuclear weapons that I lost track of Morgan."

"I understand. I do recall telling you to concentrate on the nuclear devices. Regardless, I have given the situation much thought and decided you will return to once again head North American operations. One of your first projects will be to monitor Gregori Yancy."

Rental Truck Cargo Area

"Yuri, you know we must keep her alive."

"Alive means pulse."

"Our families will suffer too if you molest her. It would be very bad."

"I am not concerned."

Joanna curled into a fetal position and pushed herself as far into a corner as possible.

"Listen to me, imbecile. I do not wish to piss away hard work in *banda* so you can have your way with hostage."

"Who will know? *Bocc* has bigger worries."

"Touch her, and I will shoot you to save me. You know what *Bocc* does to men who disobey orders. I will not be one of those men. Remember Sea Wind Bay?"

"Do not remind me."

"So, you must keep your pants on. Beat her so marks do not show."

Joanna sighed. *At least one of them wants to follow their boss's orders. Where is Jake, and how long can I stay safe with these thugs?"*

"I tell you not to do that. Why do you not listen?"

"Not to worry. She will not be able to tell if I smash her mouth...."

The next sound was a wood-stock rifle bashing someone's head and a body hitting the floor with a dull thud. The whining of tires on the highway was the only sound that remained. She sensed the guard in front of her and smelled the cabbage he had for lunch.

"*Bocc* wants to trade you for something, so I will not hurt you if you behave. This idiot is only hired...."

The sound of squealing tires drowned out his words. The truck swerved, lurched, and came to a sudden stop that threw her captor to the floor.

"What is happening? Why do we stop?" Joanna's captor demanded, as he pounded on the wall to the cab.

"*Politsiya* stop one of our trucks on highway," was the curt reply. "*Bocc* says we will soon continue, but must have weapons ready."

Consortium Headquarters

"I am puzzled, Commissioner," Gunter Wilhelm said reluctantly. "I was under the impression Yancy worked for us, yet you are ordering me to monitor him. If I may ask, to what end?"

The Commissioner was not used to being questioned by a subordinate, and a scowl darkened his face. They stared at each other across the massive desk until the Commissioner blinked and continued,

"Yancy is still an associate. However, I must balance the value of his association with us while maintaining checks and balances on his aspirations."

The Commissioner folded his hands on the desk and his face lost all expression for a moment. "I examined the inventory of the property Yancy added to the Deer Trail warehouse. We believed all records were destroyed, so I was pleased to discover you had copies on your laptop."

"I endeavor to be thorough, sir."

"Indeed, but there were discrepancies. Crates were checked in with no description of the contents. How do you explain this?"

"A few possibilities exist, sir. The most obvious would be corruption of my staff."

"Would not your second-in-command monitor such activity?"

"Yes, which leads me to believe he may have indeed been corrupted. It would explain such obvious mistakes with the inventory."

The Commissioner smiled for the first time. "I appreciate your forthright candor, and you are correct. The man apparently knew nothing of the plot to destroy the facility and became a victim himself due to avarice."

"Avarice?"

"Yes, raw greed it would seem. A deep search uncovered overseas accounts in an alias he sometimes used. They contained over two million US dollars that have remained untouched since the incident. I suppose he could still be alive, but I find the possibility remote."

"That would certainly explain much."

"Furthermore, the money originated with a shell company owned by Yancy. But enough of Yancy. I have decided to return you to your position as Director of Operations for North America."

"Yes, you said that earlier."

"I did?" The Commissioner stared at the ceiling for several moments. "Are you positive?"

Gunter grew uncomfortable with the blank look after a while. *Is it for effect, or are the rumors about his mental lapses true?*

The Commissioner shook his head as if to clear his mind. "Where was I? Oh yes, I remember now. I have a secure replacement facility in mind for you to develop as your new operations center."

Gunter waited for details.

***

Chapter 6

St. Lawrence Seaway Aboard the *SP Lee*

"Captain, the storm is getting worse," Andy said over the intercom. "Everything is lashed down tight, but we're taking on water, even with the pumps at full open." He heard a child's laughter in the background.

"Would be better if ship is heavier," Gorsky replied. "On the other hand, weight would keep us deeper in water and slow our progress. Company is strict about schedule, so face into wind and sail on."

I-80 West of South Bend, Indiana

"Again, Director?" Jake said as he answered the sat phone.

"No, Agent Thomas, this is Dave Stotts, a comm-sat tech in the Situation Room."

"The Director's usually the one who calls me on my sat phone."

"I understand, but we finally convinced him to go get some sleep. I'm the Duty Officer tonight, and I have an update for you on Yancy. Satellite scans show the subjects' radios have broken into two groups. One appears to be standing alone, while several others are grouped together a few miles away. I'm not sure what that means, but thought you'd like to know."

"Thanks, Dave. Don't know why they would split up, either. If one broke down, you'd think the others would stay with it. They would all be together if they stopped for the night, so what's going on? Bob, you got any thoughts?"

"Sorry, I'm clueless, too."

"Anything else, Dave?"

"Satellite data shows the lone radio has been dark for a while. It's got to mean something, but I can't figure out exactly what. Anyway, it looks like they're only thirty miles or so ahead of you."

"At least we're closing in on them. Thanks again, Dave."

"You're welcome, sir, and best of luck."

Jake ended the call, leaned back in the seat, and let out an expressive sigh. All he wanted to do was close his eyes and sleep as long as his aching body wanted. But that would not happen anytime soon. "We can't lose them."

"What makes you think we're gonna lose them?" Uncle Bob replied. "We're far from out of the game. Besides, it's getting late. Maybe they've stopped for the night, and we can sneak up on them."

"We can only hope."

Consortium Headquarters, Switzerland

"As I said earlier, I am restoring you to your former position," the Commissioner said to Gunter Wilhelm. "I will, however, send an assistant to help you."

"I do not require a nanny." Gunter leaned slightly forward. "I left the Deer Trail Site because I thought you ordered me to."

"Yes, Wilhelm, which is why you still breathe. I would not hesitate to end your employment and your life if I thought you were disloyal. My sincere desire is for complete trust to be restored over time. The assistant will be withdrawn when I am assured of your complete loyalty."

Gunter leaned back in the chair and forced a smile of acceptance. "As you wish, Commissioner. Where will my new operations center be?"

"An oil refinery on the East Bay of Houston, Texas was shut down for updates some years ago. The former owners ceased renovating it when oil prices sank."

The Commissioner swiveled his chair to the side to look out wall-sized windows at the alpine meadow beyond. "We acquired the property a few years ago. It sits between a major highway and the Houston Ship Channel. Improved perimeter fencing and security, as well as constant truck traffic will camouflage our operation."

"When do you expect me to be on site?"

"You will leave once our conversation is complete," the Commissioner said as took a sip from a crystal goblet. He swiveled his chair back to face Gunter. "Innate trust is difficult to achieve in our line of work and easily lost. Do not fail me, Mister Wilhelm."

"Thank you, Commissioner, I shall not." *I'd be dead if he knew about the listening devices I installed in his office and the boardroom.*

"Very well, then. My secretary has a file for you with necessary information, including personnel, facility layout, and passcodes. It also includes account numbers and passwords for funds in encrypted accounts. For your eyes only."

"Of course, Commissioner." Gunter stood and turned to walk out of the office.

"Godspeed, Mister Wilhelm."

Gunter thought he heard the Commissioner speak and turned around. The Director of one of the most powerful intelligence-gathering organizations in the world was mumbling incoherently to himself.

Gunter gently closed the door.

I-80 Eastbound on the Indiana Toll Road

"BSOG-1, this is Comm-1. They sure aren't using their radios much."

"Probably just as bored as we are, but we still need to monitor them closely. We're too close to lose them now."

"I'll keep my eyes and ears glued to the dials. We'll catch up in no time, I'm sure of it."

"I'm counting on it. Make sure we don't slip past them somehow and end up in the lead."

"Actually, we have some backup on that. I got an update on satellite intel from the National Reconnaissance Office. Their tracking system also shows the subjects were eastbound on I-80, and still ahead of us."

Jake spoke tight-lipped into the radio, "All units, let's go catch these guys." He stared ahead with determination and with his hands firmly on the wheel.

Jake was startled a few minutes later by a blast of static from the radio.

The voice of Senior Agent Jay Johansen burst forth, "BSOG-4 here. Got some bad news, Boss. We are running on fumes. Didn't have time to fill up after the raid yesterday. Hate to say it, but either we stop now, or end up pushing these rigs down the road by hand."

"Copy that, Four. All units, give me a sit-rep on fuel." All were low. "We'll stop at the next service plaza. Comm-1, have somebody monitor the equipment while you take a break. I don't want to lose them."

"Roger that, Boss. I'm on top of it."

"Good. Next stop is one mile. Do a fast in and out. Gas, bathroom, and grab something to eat on the way out."

"Hey, Boss, Comm-1. The Situation Room says satellite shows perps stopped near Elkhart with no movement for over ten minutes. Maybe they bedded down for the night. By the way, we pulled into the gas station right behind you."

Fifteen minutes later Jake said to Uncle Bob, "I'll ask the Director to contact local LEO's for backup."

"Good idea. We can always use a few extra trained hands."

Jake spoke into the radio, "Everybody a go?" All units confirmed. "Okay then, let's hit the road."

Indiana Toll Road

"Vasily, do you see propane tank farm by exit?" Yancy asked over their comm units.

"*Da, Boss,* is very big."

"Use RPG to destroy biggest propane tank in middle. Will create major distraction for *politsiya*. But you must wait until after we pass, for I do not wish to be blown to pieces."

"*Da, Boss.* Explosion will be seen for many kilometers."

"That is my wish. Tank will break others open to keep *politsiya* busy for hours."

Bristol Post, Indiana State Police

"Now the fun part starts. Damn paperwork," TT muttered as he and Hubbard guided the handcuffed men into the Toll Road Post.

"Sure, but think of all the overtime we'd miss if it wasn't for guys like this. Helped pay for my fishing cabin up in Grayling."

Hubbard held the glass double doors open and followed into the harsh glare of bright fluorescent lights in the lobby. "Let's put these bozos in Interrogation One and Two and see if we can figure out what's going on."

TT led his charge down the gray-tiled hallway to a room at the end.

Hubbard guided his suspect into a room across the hall. "You sure I can't get you something to drink, like a soda, or coffee?" Hubbard asked the driver of the rental truck. "I went through the truck for your real identities and came up with zilch...."

"What is this zilch?"

It was the first words the suspect had uttered since they left the scene of the traffic stop.

Hubbard smiled and hoped the guy would finally open up. "Means I didn't find out who you are. We ran the serial numbers on your weapons and came up with zilch, even though they've been converted to fully automatic. The ATF Tax Stamp should have popped up, but it didn't. It's either listed under an alias, or illegally converted. Which is it?"

Hubbard waited for the reply he knew probably would not be forthcoming, and continued, "All right then, if that's the way you want to play it, guess I'll read you your Miranda Rights. Then, I'll ask you one last time to answer my questions. If you don't, I will arrest you. Best start working right now on the story you'll tell the judge in the morning."

The driver sat back in the chair and glared at the obviously frustrated trooper.

Indiana Toll Road

Vasily grinned as he unpacked the Rifle Propelled Grenade from its case. "This will be much fun," he said to the other men.

He loaded a round and took careful aim at the largest propane tank. A dozen five-hundred-gallon tanks surrounded two ten-thousand-gallon distribution tanks. Vasily surveyed the peaceful tranquility of the early morning scene as if in a trance. He stood still for a moment and took a deep breath of the crisp air.

"Rock and roll," Vasily screamed as he braced himself and fired. The round left its launcher with a jolt. Stabilizing fins folded out as the rocket hurtled toward one of the 10,000-gallon tanks in a deadly spiral.

The ensuing fireball and massive concussive wave that followed blew Vasily to the ground a dozen feet behind him. "Holy Mother of God!" was all he could say to the henchmen who were also knocked down.

Vasily quickly rolled over and got to his feet. One of his men looked at him with a mixture of shock and amazement. The man's lips moved.

"I cannot hear you," Vasily said as he pointed to his head. He yelled as loudly as he could, "Explosion rings in my ears. I think maybe we are too close, eh?" Vasily laughed and the man joined in, despite not being able to hear what was said.

Bristol State Police Post

Hubbard motioned Taets out of the room across the hall. "Get anything out of your guy?"

"Not a peep. Hasn't even asked to go to the bathroom."

"Mirandize him, and I'll ask Top about a search warrant for their truck."

The young trooper from the front desk sauntered down the hallway toward them. "Top said to wrap it up. Your suspects are going to County."

"County? That's good. I'll be glad to wash my hands of them and go home."

He moved both men to the same room. "Okay, boys, I guess this is it. You're both going to jail as John Doe's. It's almost 5 AM, and by noon I'll have a judge's okay to search the truck. Sure you don't want to make any statements?"

Both men stared at the ceiling in silence.

"Suit yourselves. It would save a lot of time and trouble if you'd identify yourselves. But, since you seem to have a case of lockjaw, we'll turn this over to detectives to investigate. For now, some of our fine day shift Troopers will take you to the county jail. You'll stay there until we figure out who the heck you are. I get to do another two hours of paperwork, thank you very much."

The two prisoners looked at each other, and a hint of a smile crossed their faces.

Hubbard took note of the interaction. "You two sure you don't want to talk?"

"*Nyet.*"

"No."

"It's your funeral, so have it your way."

***

Chapter 7

Indiana Toll Road

The morning sun slowly chased darkness toward the west as it had from the beginning of time. Today it had help from the propane depot a scant hundred feet from the heavily traveled interstate. Five-hundred-gallon propane tanks strewn over the landscape randomly exploded, sending brilliant yellow and red plumes hundreds of feet skyward. Small tanks skittered away like unguided rockets, and liquid propane hissed from broken safety valves.

"We must go before other tanks explode," Vasily told his driver. "And before *Politsiya* get here."

They got into the SUV and pulled onto the road to follow the route of the troopers and Yancy.

Vasily grabbed the two-way radio. *"Da, Bocc,* is done as you order. No one will use Toll Road for very long time because of damage to pavement."

"Good," Yancy replied. "Federal agents who pursue us face huge obstacle. We will soon have my truck back. Your good work will be richly rewarded."

Vasily grinned as he settled back into the comfortable leather seat. *Is good to please Bocc*

.

DEA Office, Indianapolis, Indiana

"DEA, Fort Wayne, how may I help you?"

"I'd like to make an anonymous tip."

"Please hold while I transfer you."

"Intel Duty Desk."

"Yeah, okay, look, a yellow Penske cargo truck with a ton of dope was stopped in Bristol about an hour ago."

"A ton of dope, you say? Any particular kind?"

"Cocaine in five-kilo bundles wrapped in gray duct tape. You know, that kind of dope."

"How do you know all this?"

"Because my neighbor forced me to help load it. Said he'd burn my house down with my family inside if I didn't. Turns out he's a major dealer. I don't think we're going to be friends anymore, and if you do your job, we won't be neighbors either."

"How do you know the truck was stopped?"

"Like, I'm sitting on my back patio just now when my neighbor throws a half-full bottle of beer at my fence and breaks one of the boards. Glass shatters all over hell and creation. Then he starts yelling at a police scanner about how the stupid State Police got his load. You gotta put him away so the neighborhood can be safe again."

"And your name, sir?"

"John...John Hancock. But the more I think about it, maybe this isn't such a great idea. He could come back at me and my family if he finds out I ratted him out...."

"We have programs to protect you."

"You mean like that Witness Protection thing? So you're saying I should rip my kids out of school and move to Kneejerk, Montana, or some hole-in-the-wall place? I don't think so." Jack Morgan smiled as he hung up the payphone. "That should throw a monkey wrench into Yancy's plans," he said to Wild Bill, who nodded in reply.

Speedway Gas Station Parking Lot, Bristol, Indiana

"Take five men with you," Yancy said to Sasha as they stood next to an SUV in the parking lot of the brightly lit convenience store. A light breeze chased a paper cup across the blacktop. "Drop two men off at State Police Post to get truck back. Take three with you to attack *politsiya* van. Bring my men back at any cost."

"*Da, Bocc*. I use two vehicles?"

"*Nyet*. Take only one SUV. I will continue to Toledo, Ohio. Attack when police van is isolated. Of course, leave no witnesses. Meet me at address in Toledo."

"*Da, Bocc*."

"But first have two men find hotels where people who move long distance stay to exchange license plates. They will continue to Toledo with cargo truck, while you get my men back."

"*Da, Bocc*...is no problem. I take no risks."

"Good. I have someone watching State Police Post. They say my men are inside. Truck is in lot with next to building.

They must take back truck before police see inside."

"I will not fail, *Bocc*."

"*Da*, you have been faithful. Is why I trust you. I must continue to Toledo to keep schedule. You get big bonus when job is done, for trusted men are hard to find in this business."

Two of the mercenaries walked by. One overheard the conversation and asked if Yancy wanted anything from the store. Yancy grunted in reply, scowled, and stared at the man who averted his eyes and walked away.

Sasha and crew departed west in the heavily tinted SUV ten minutes later. Yancy's convoy turned eastbound toward an entrance back onto I-80. The glow of uncontrolled propane fires painted the sky tangerine orange and hot pink. Emergency vehicles rushed past them in the opposite direction with lights flashing and sirens screaming.

Yancy smiled.

Oil Refinery, East Bay, Houston, Texas

"Howdy, Mister Wilhelm. I'm Jim Ballard, manager of the GoldStar Refinery." The tall, lanky man wearing a scratched white hard hat with a company logo on the front extended a firm handshake. "How was your trip?"

"Very well, thank you." Gunter gazed out at a complex of towers, tanks, twisting pipes, and buildings that supported a variety of operations that were a mystery to him. The rotten-egg smell of sulfuric acid hung heavily in the humid Gulf Coast air, and mixed with crude oil, grease, and rust. It was quite a contrast from the sparkling clean air of the Swiss Alps. "How long have you worked here?"

Ballard grinned. "Seems like my whole life. Got here five years ago to mothball it, and now we're getting ready to fire her back up. That's the nature of the oil business."

"As the new owners, our company wants the facility to be updated and ready to process crude oil as soon as possible. Within reasonable cost parameters, of course. I intend to rely heavily on you, James...."

"Please call me Jim. We're pretty informal around here. The majority of my men have worked in refineries in one place or another all over the world. With the proper motivation, they are willing to do whatever it takes to get back up to speed. Now one thing I have found that motivates men is a healthy bonus."

Gunter glared at Jim. "How would keeping their jobs suit them? Would that motivate them?"

"Well, um, yes, sir, of course. I'm just bringing up questions they'll likely ask, so I already have the answers. We're talking about hiring a lot of new people in a short time. The oil business is a small community, and we wouldn't want word to get out that we're a little on the stingy side. Besides, I like to be straight with potential hires right from the git-go."

"I understand and will take that into account as I go over a complete plan with you this evening...."

"Tonight? My daughter's got a playoff game in her softball league that starts at Seven O'clock."

Gunter stared at the ground for a moment and then back up at Jim. "Have I not made myself clear? I need you one hundred percent on board with this project. May I count on you?"

"Let me make myself clear then," Jim replied with a steely stare. "I took the mothball operation five years ago to be near my family. The pay is lower, but I figured it was a tradeoff since family means everything to me. We'll need to seriously renegotiate my contract if you plan to tie up most of my time."

"So, you expect to enrich yourself at company expense?"

"Didn't say that, but a man's time is a precious resource."

"I agree. What, exactly, are you proposing, vis-à-vis your salary?"

"I currently make a hundred fifty thou a year for watching over a sleepy little operation. A turnaround like you're propos...."

"Turnaround?"

"Taking an operation from dormant to fully functioning. It's a whole 'nother ballgame. Seems like you're asking me to turn this place around, and then run it. Am I right?"

"That is what our employers wish to occur."

"A three-year contract at one million a year would work for me, or eight hundred thousand a year with a stepped bonus based upon a completion schedule would also work."

"Would one point two five million a year with bonuses be adequate?"

"Wait, hold on just a minute. Do I need to get my hearing checked, or are you offering me ten times what I currently make?"

"I am, with stipulations, of course. For instance, you must sign a non-disclosure agreement."

"NDAs in the oil business are common for upper management. What else?"

"My employers will be conducting other operations on the refinery grounds. They, too would be included in the NDA."

"I don't have a problem with that, so long as they're aboveboard."

"The Consortium Group simply needs to protect proprietary information."

"Something that is also common in the oil business. So, long story short, we're on the same page?"

"It appears we are. Now, I understand my short notice request for your presence tonight was ill-advised. Shall we meet back here at, say, nine in the morning?"

"I'm usually in my office at seven, so it don't matter to me. I'll have the coffee on and ready."

"I'm a tea drinker, if you could accommodate me."

"I'll clue my secretary in."

"Please tell her I will bring my own if she can have hot water and sugar available. I do not take cream or honey."

"Sounds good. My office is in the building behind us, first floor behind the reception desk. Do you need a ride to your hotel?"

"Thank you, but no. I have a car and driver."

Indiana State Police Post, Bristol, Indiana

"Hey, TT, we just got the search warrant. Let's go take a little peek inside the truck."

"Sure thing, Bill. It's gotta be packed with a ton of drugs, right?" TT replied as they walked toward the impound. "Where the heck did the tow truck drop it? I don't see it anywhere."

"Me neither. I mean, how do you miss a big banana-colored truck?"

The troopers walked around the enclosure to the only gate. "Uh, oh, look at that." Taets pointed to a broken chain and lock on the ground.

"Who the hell breaks into a State Police impound yard? Takes a big stink'n pair, I tell you. Let's go ask Brighton if he knows anything."

"Brighton?"

"Fresh-faced newbie on the front desk. Supposed to tell the tow truck driver where to put it. We can also look at camera footage and put an ATL out on it."

"You're the man with the plan."

"No, I didn't watch the tow truck drop the perp's truck," Brighton replied to their question. "He brought the key back and swore he locked the yard up tight. I'm not in trouble, am I?"

Taets and Hubbard exchanged looks.

"No, you did everything by the book," Hubbard said. "Tell you what, why don't you call the tow truck...."

"He won't have time," the First Sergeant said as he rushed into the office. "Just got a call from Dispatch. We got a major incident at Green's Propane. One of their big tanks blew up and is raining fire down all over the place. About a mile of the toll road is shut down with dozens of vehicles trapped. We need every Tom, Dick, and Harry to work traffic and containment."

"What about us?" Taets asked. "You want us out there?"

"Yes, but first I need you to take your prisoners to County. I don't want anybody tied up babysitting them here."

"Yes, Top. We'll call after they book them in."

"Good. Can't imagine what happened to the tanks. Never had a problem with them before."

"As the old saying goes, there's always a first time," Hubbard offered.

"True, but I wonder if your prisoners were somehow involved," Top replied.

"Don't see how, but they were traveling in a convoy. I guess only time will tell."

"Time is what we're in short supply of at the moment," Top said. "That, and manpower."

***

Chapter 8

I-80, Eastbound, West of Bristol, Indiana

"Good Lord, Jake, where did the fireball come from all of a sudden?" Uncle Bob exclaimed.

"No way to tell. Might just be hell from the looks of it," Jake replied. "Could be a tanker truck on the Toll Road, or a major gas line next to the highway from the looks of it. Biggest I've ever seen outside a combat zone."

Bob stomped on the brakes as taillights flared in front of them. The vehicle came to a screeching halt in the middle of the roadway. One fireball after another rocketed into the sky a scant few miles ahead. Moments later their SUV was rocked by a massive concussion. Brilliant reds and oranges in the rolling black mushroom cloud billowed upward and swirled out in all directions.

"Can't be one of our nukes," Jake said, "or we'd have vaporized."

The 2-way radios roared to life with the rest of the convoy talking all at once.

"Drive slowly ahead, Bob. Let's see if the road is passable."

Bob let the SUV roll forward until they encountered a barricade of stalled vehicles. "Not much we can do to help, what with the pavement broken up and disabled cars blocking the way. We won't be going that way anytime soon."

"How far back was the last exit?"

"Ten miles, more or less, Boss."

"All units, cross the median here and go back to the Elkhart exit. We'll take State Road 120 eastbound to catch up to them."

"Director?" Jake asked as he answered the satellite phone. "What's going on?"

"I wanted to pass along some new intel on Yancy. The Indiana State Police Post in Bristol, Indiana reported they pulled over a stolen rental truck early this morning. Two men, possibly Russian, carrying fake California drivers' licenses. The truck was reported stolen out of Deer Trail, Colorado."

"Deer Trail? Are you kidding me?"

"Nope. Plates had been switched. Suspects were armed with automatic weapons and a ton of ammo. Troopers also confiscated a portable two-way radio."

"Please tell me we got it."

"Not quite yet, but I am sending an agent there to retrieve it. Suspects are being transported to the Elkhart County Jail. I am getting a Writ of Habeas Corpus to take custody of the prisoners."

"That's great news, but think about it, we can be there before the DC agent gets off the ground. Where's the jail?"

"Goshen, Indiana." Banner laughed. "Reminds me of the old TV Show *Mayberry RFD.*"

"RFD?"

"Rural Free Delivery. Old guy name for a backwater town like the place where I grew up."

"I'm looking at the map, Director. It's less than an hour away. We'll head there to find out what their plans were."

"Sounds like a better idea for you to pick up the radio and prisoners. But from what I understand, the radio is at the State Police Post in Bristol. That means two stops for you unless you want me to get it picked up and taken to the jail."

"Thanks, Director, but I'd rather do it myself. Won't be happy until I get my hands on it."

"I will tell my agent to stay here in DC and ask the Bristol Post Commander to have the radio ready for you."

"Thanks. I feel like we're a lot closer to recovering the nukes and Joanna."

"Call me when you have the suspects and radio in hand."

F.E. Warren Air Force Base, Wyoming

Star Jackman rolled her head slowly in a wide circle and grimaced in pain. She glanced around the gym to make sure no one could hear her talking to Licia. "I'm still aching from being thrown across the room yesterday. Gwen's working us too hard. I don't know if I can take much more."

Licia nodded. "I understand, but after the campground attack, there's no such thing as being too ready. Sure, we've got guards around us all the time, but we can't always depend on them to get to us in time. We have got to be able to be our own first line of defense if the bad guys come at us again. Joanna is still missing, and they don't even know if she's alive. If they can get to her, they can definitely get to us."

"Ladies," Gwen said as she strolled toward them while tapping a clipboard with a pen. "Let's go over what we've covered so far. One of the first things I told you is you need to be ready for the unexpected. Situational awareness says you need to keep someone from sneaking up on you. As the old saying goes, plan for the worst, and hope for the best. Remember, do something, do anything."

Star rolled her eyes.

Gwen's eyebrows went up. "Am I boring you?" she asked.

"No, well, not exactly. It's just that you keep repeating the same things over and over. We have heard you say to 'Do something, do anything' at least a hundred times."

"Actually, I was shooting for a thousand. Years of experience from a lot of people went into the design of this course. And one thing that sticks out like a sore thumb is repetition. There isn't time during an attack to formulate a response. Calculated actions must occur reflexively."

"Huh?"

"It means you've got to respond without thinking about it," Licia said.

"Yeah, I get it…I guess," Star replied.

"Which is why I keep going over it time and time again," Gwen said with a sigh of exasperation. "I'm trying to teach you a whole lot of material in a very short time. I've said it a hundred times, but it's true, ladies. You need to react to danger in a heartbeat, and when you least expect it."

"I think that makes it a hundred and one times," Licia said with a smile.

Gwen returned the smile. "The key is repeating the same movements over and over again to create muscle memory."

"Yes, and we really appreciate what you're trying to do," Licia replied. "But you have to understand how stressful this is for us. Just knowing there are people out there who want to hurt us is kind of terrifying."

"I know, and I try to keep that in mind. Honestly, I don't understand why these people keep coming at you. Our debriefing says you don't seem to know anything about their operation. Unless there's some detail you may have missed, I'm mystified."

"We wondered that, too. We racked our brains and can't figure out what it might be."

"Besides, what could we possibly know that would light such a fire under these guys?" Star interjected. "We've been through every detail of our time in Sea Wind Bay minute-by-minute. Nothing jumps out. So why do they keep coming after us?"

"That's the million-dollar question. Hopefully, we'll find the answer. But for now, it's time for strikes and blocking practice."

The girls groaned in unison.

***

Chapter 9

Indiana State Police Post, Bristol, Indiana

"Top, I have a BOLO I think you'll want to see," Taets said as he rapped on the door frame and entered the commander's office.

"What's it about? I'm kind of busy going through surveillance footage of the impound yard. Two men in dark clothes used bolt cutters on the gate chain. Had on ball caps and looked down a lot to hide their faces. Knew exactly what they were doing."

"Which means this BOLO could be related. Warns of a heavily armed and dangerous group out of Chicago who may be headed east. Says there was a shootout in a southside warehouse two days ago. What's interesting is it didn't come from the Chicago PD," TT said.

"From the state?"

"Nope, and that's what's strange. Came out of NSA Headquarters in DC."

Top forcefully exhaled. "Well, that is different. Okay, let's put two and two together. The two we stopped last night were driving a stolen truck and heavily armed. Did you run the serial numbers on the weapons?"

"Yes, through NCIC & IDAC's. This BOLO gives a point of contact and says to call if we have any info. Should I call, since you're going over the footage?"

"Yeah, call and give them what we have so far. I want to clear this up ASAP so we can concentrate on other things, like the propane depot."

"Will do pronto, Top."

GoldStar Refinery

"I was under the impression the Consortium Group was an investment fund," Jim Ballard said as he sipped coffee from a porcelain mug with the GoldStar logo. "Didn't realize they were oil men."

"Your first impression is correct," Gunter Wilhelm replied. "They are not oil men, per se. However, due diligence required them to investigate, so they hired some of the best minds in the business to evaluate the refinery and formulate this plan."

"Charts, graphs, and studies from across the globe. They must have spent a fortune."

"I believe you have a saying in America that it takes money to make money."

"That's as true as the day is long." Jim took a long sip of coffee. "I detect an accent. Does that mean you're not from here, and not an oilman?"

"Where I am from is not important, nor is my background. Shall we continue?"

"Yes, Boss, by all means," Jim replied, and hesitated before continuing, "After all, this is your dog and pony show. I haven't figured out if I'm a dog or a pony. I was just trying to get the lay of the land."

Gunter stared out the office window for a moment. "Which, I am sure, is why you are successful. Allow me to clarify your second assumption by confirming I am not an oilman. However, I am experienced in upper-level management and have done rather well working with men who were more than a little rough around the edges."

"Glad to hear that," Jim replied. "Most of my crew live what could be called ordinary lives. You know, nine-to-five jobs. Houses in the suburbs, fishing, and barbeques on the weekends. They are salt of the earth types who work hard to support their families. Their goal is to retire after thirty years on the job and fish full time for fun, which is actually an excuse to drink beer. On the other hand, I do have a few hell-raising womanizers who drink hard and like to fight at the drop of a hat. It takes all kinds. My job is to maintain balance and keep them in line. In other words, to remind them of their goals."

"I see. It would seem you have good knowledge of your men. Allow me to clarify another point. Our employers do not wish to start over with a new manager, which is why they will consent to your salary requests. Our attorneys will draw up the contract if you are still interested."

"Sure am, and look forward to working with you. Just tell me what you want done and put it out of your mind."

"That is the dynamic I desire. Shall we start by going over the basics?"

"Like I said, it's your show."

"Man, I can't believe it's lunchtime already," Jim noted as his stomach growled. "Three hours just to go over the basic plan."

Gunter smiled for the first time. "As I said, the plan to reopen the refinery was concocted by experts. They were very thorough."

"Can't argue with that. Looks like they dotted every I and crossed every T. One thing they didn't spell out is your part in the operation. Where do you fit in, and where will your offices be? We have plenty of room in this building, so you can stake out your territory."

"I was curious as to when you might broach the subject," Gunter replied. "There is too much traffic in this building to suit me. The refinery has a Research and Development building, does it not?"

"Sure does. Tucked away in an isolated corner of the complex over by the bay. Not exactly prime real estate."

"Yes, but it would afford excellent privacy. From what I gather, it's not fully utilized."

"Now there's an understatement if I ever heard one. Sixty thousand square feet on three floors, not counting two service subbasements. R&D uses less than ten thousand, all of it on the first floor. The ship terminal originally used the rest years ago to unload small coastal freighters. We dropped the freighter operations years ago as the refinery operation grew. Security was too much of an issue. Today, crude comes in by pipeline or truck. Super tankers also deliver it out in the Gulf at docking terminals. Comes to the refinery by underwater pipeline."

"Sounds logical," Gunter replied.

"Anybody who visited the building in the past had to go through four layers of security designed to protect the tankers. Won't be a problem with your people since they'll be vetted employees. They will only have to check in through the Northeast gate and park in the lot next to your building."

"They will have direct access to the building then?"

"Not quite. They'll need to pass through personnel gates to sign in and have their security credentials scanned. Except for senior people like you, of course. You'll go through a gate with key card access further down by the executive parking area. It's right next to the building and covered to protect your vehicle from fly ash…."

Gunter interrupted Jim, "What is this fly ash, and why must you protect vehicles?"

"It's acidic and can damage paint over time. Maybe you didn't notice, but we have two drive-through car washes on site. Not the full operations you might be used to, but they spray detergent and rinse employees' cars for free."

"I did not notice car washes. My driver sees to the care and maintenance of my vehicles. I believe the R&D building will suffice and wish to examine it."

"Thought you'd never ask. I had a hard hat made with your name on it."

Gunter examined the front of the hat. "Thank you, this is a first for me, and a nice gesture."

"You're more'n welcome, but it's no gesture. OSHA requires it."

"OSHA?"

"Occupational Safety Health Administration, just one of many Federal regulatory agencies I deal with every day," Jim replied as he held the exit door open. "My golf cart is right outside the door."

"I suppose that is the most efficient means of transport within the facility," Gunter said as he settled into the plastic bench seat of the utility vehicle. It was parked under a solid cover in spaces designated for management."

"I ordered a custom cart for your personal use. It should be here within a week or so."

"Thank you. Are you the owner of the Harley Davidson motorcycle in the next stall?"

"Sure am. Use it to commute. It's one of my most prized possessions."

"Understandable. It is a magnificent machine. I am not familiar with the acquisition of a vehicle such as this. Were you required to place a special order to get the Mint Green color with the Shamrock and Leprechaun painted on the fuel tank?"

"Actually, it's Emerald Green. Harley doesn't carry that color, so I ordered it in white and had a local guy do the paintwork. I call the bar area of my garage at home the Angry Leprechaun. The bike sits in it near the pool table."

Gunter had a thoughtful expression as he spoke, "I have a parlor in my house for entertaining guests, but it does not have a motorcycle. Perhaps I should consider acquiring one."

"Each to his own, as they say," Jim replied as he navigated the cart along gravel paths surrounded by pipes and tanks. "Although, I imagine a billiard table might be more to your liking. You know, better for your image."

"You might be surprised."

Jim stopped the cart a few minutes later and pointed toward a series of tanks, and four-foot diameter pipes mounted just off the ground, "This is the initial feed system. Makes no difference whether crude comes in through the gulf terminal, the dock, or over the land-based pipeline. The crude in the feed system is heated by the southeastern Texas sun. It's sifted, filtered, and turned into various end products. Everything from gasoline in various grades, to chemicals used in everyday life. You know, like automotive fluids and coatings, to adhesives and cleaners. We also produce polymers that are used in plastics."

"How long has it been since crude oil was fully processed here?"

"Just before she was put into mothballs. About five years ago. I've been keeping maintenance up on everything, but we haven't run crude through since then. I'm eager to fire everything up again."

"Very well. You must keep me up to date as the startup progresses, so I may inform our employers. You should also tell your crew I will not tolerate anyone who does not contribute their best effort."

"I keep them on a pretty tight rein." Jim saw Gunter's reaction and shifted gears. "But I'll let my men know...."

"Our men, if you don't mind. They work for you, and you, in turn, work for me. Forgive me if that sounds a bit harsh, but I have worked with men who would kill to have my job." *And died trying to replace me.* "I do not intend to give them an opportunity. Now, shall we get back to the business at hand? How long will it take to start processing crude?"

"Well, I'd need to check a few key things, but as a guess...."

"I do not like guesses, Mister Ballard. Please use the rest of the day to lay out a schedule of how long it will take to get back to full processing. Include test runs, and a timeline with key target dates listed. Now, please continue the tour so I may see the R&D building we discussed."

"Like I said, you're the boss."

***

Chapter 10

Elkhart County Jail, Goshen, Indiana

Uncle Bob wheeled the extended black Suburban up to the sallyport on the west side of the four-story red brick jail. He drove as close as possible to an intercom system mounted on a dull-brown steel post with numerous scrapes of various colors.

Bob stretched to reach the bent post to push the intercom button. There was a lengthy pause, and he turned to Jake, "This is as bad as the drive-through window at McDonalds."

"Can I help you?" a tinny voice finally responded.

"I hope so. We're here to pick up a couple of prisoners."

"Yeah, I got a message here. I need to check your ID's," the voice in the speaker monotoned. "Hold them up to the camera."

Bob held both ID's up to the camera.

"What a joke," Jake whispered. "No way they can read them with this old equipment. They're just going through the motions to cover their asses."

"Excuse me?" the tinny voice said. "Did you say something about our security? We don't have the resources you high and mighty Feds have, but we do the best we can with what we have."

"Uh, you must have misunderstood my partner," Uncle Bob quickly answered. "He was talking about another case we're working on. We appreciate your help on a case with national security implications."

"Let me guess, all your cases have national security implications, right?" Sarcasm dripped through the speaker. "Nice way to bloat a budget."

"Believe me, this case is more important than you could ever imagine."

"I'm sure it is, but I get my fill of it from you people. Whatever, you're cleared to go in." The overhead door rattled and clanked up to allow access to the secure sallyport.

A uniformed deputy with hands on hips and a double-chinned jaw jutted out waited as Bob slowly pulled in. The thirty-pound duty belt around his ample waist sported an empty holster, speed loaders, pepper spray, handcuffs, and a radio. A gut that appeared to weigh even more hung over the well-worn belt.

"Need to see your ID's," His cold welcome echoed off drab concrete walls and floor that lent a hollow quality to his words.

Jake and Bob held up their ID's while the deputy examined them. "Names match the memo I got. I'm sure you're familiar with the drill, but I need to recite our rules. Anything that could be used as a weapon is forbidden and must be held in one of our lockboxes."

Two-dozen steel boxes with chipped green paint were recessed into the sidewall. Keys dangled from open doors to indicate which were available.

"Put everything inside, lock it and take the key. Retrieve your property when you leave, but don't forget to leave the key, or we bill your agency fifty bucks."

As they complied with his order. Jake leaned over and whispered to Bob, "Typical king of the castle, right?"

"For sure," Bob replied as they stood. "We're ready."

The deputy pressed the mike button on his radio and stared at a camera. "Open-12." He nodded to Jake and Bob. "Follow me."

A reinforced box in the doorjamb made a thumping grinding noise as the concrete-filled steel door electrically unlocked. The deputy leaned backward and used his considerable bulk to pull the heavy door. "I'll take you to the OIC of the shift."

"Are the two men who were arrested by the State Police ready to go with us?" Jake asked the deputy.

"Don't know what you're talking about, officer. I was told to come and get you, and that's exactly what I'm doing."

Jake and Uncle Bob exchanged glances. "Actually, it's Agent," Jake replied

Fifty paces later the deputy held the door marked "Officer in Charge" open while the agents entered. "Here they are, Sergeant."

Jake could not tell if the note of disdain was directed at them or the slight figure sitting behind a worn metal desk with a chipped gray linoleum top. "I'm Agent Thomas, and this is Agent Onkst. We're here to...."

"Well now, isn't that just typical? We don't hear a word from you Feds for over a month, and all of a sudden the place is crawling with you," the sergeant said in a voice that sounded like a cross between Barney Fife and Donald Duck.

He took a puff from a menthol cigarette and continued, "You snap your fingers and expect us to jump. Plus, I don't appreciate the high and mighty tone your boss used with me."

Jake shrugged his shoulders. "I have no idea what you're talking about. Far as I know, my boss only talked to the Sheriff."

The sergeant set the cigarette down in an ashtray from the National Sheriff's Convention the year before in New Orleans. "Wait, does that mean you're not from the DEA in Indianapolis?"

"Absolutely not. We're with the NSA...."

"NSA? Why are you sticking your noses into an illegal arms bust? Doesn't make any sense. What's really going on?"

"Sorry, it's a matter of national security."

"It's always national security…."

Jake interrupted, "Hey, I don't know about always, but take my word for it, you don't want to be on the short end of the stick on this one."

"Whatever, but it really doesn't matter since the suspects aren't in my jail. The sheriff stopped the booking and wants to see you in his office, pronto. Third door down the hall on the left."

"Why would he turn the prisoners away?" Uncle Bob asked before Jake could.

"Guess you'll have to ask him. Third door down the hall on the left. Now, unless you have something else, I need to get back to running the jail." He tapped a cigarette out of a pack. "Gotta quit smoking these things. They going to kill me someday. What, you two aren't gone yet?"

Jake started to make an obscene gesture but stopped. "Good idea. Can't stand the smell in here anyway." He watched the smug expression on the sergeant's face change to anger and quickly added, "I'm allergic to cigarette smoke."

Uncle Bob pulled Jake into the hall. "Come on, Boss, we need to figure out what's going on here."

The high-pitched voice of the OIC echoed in the hallway, "Like I said...."

Jake finished the sentence, "Third door down the hall on the left."

"Not much to say," a rotund Sheriff Wilson said. "Your boss and the ATF chief got into a pissing match on a three-way conference call with me. I learned a long time ago not to get involved in inter-agency spats."

"Director Banner doesn't usually give up that fast," Jake said. "I can't imagine why he would on this case, given the national security…."

"…issues," Wilson interrupted. "Yeah, heard that from them, too. Got the message loud and clear. As I said, I try not to get between two major DC players. It'd be like throwing a bacon-wrapped kitten into a cage with two pit bulls. So, I backed off, and they settled it between themselves. It's out of my hands, and your suspects are on the way back to the State Police Post in Bristol."

Uncle Bob stood and put his hand on his team leader's shoulder. "Doesn't look like there's much we can do here, Boss. Then how about we head on over to Bristol?"

"Exactly what I was thinking."

GoldStar Refinery

Jim pointed to the front of a nondescript building with a personnel gate that stood open and unguarded. The unmistakable smells of an industrial harbor drifted in from behind it. Rotted fish, bilge water and discarded fuel created a nauseous stew of sickening smells.

"This would be my building?" Gunter remarked as their footsteps echoed on tile floor of the lobby.

"Yes, sir. It's empty now, but R&D will move back in to resume their work in preparation for the turnaround. That includes product development, research, and packaging."

"Packaging?"

"Even though we are primarily a wholesale operation, branding is important to success in a competitive market. It retains current customers and attracts new clients."

"Indeed. I intend to jointly oversee the R&D operations, as well as my own projects. This should quite nicely fit my purposes." *With the addition of upgraded surveillance equipment, fiber optic communications, and heavy steel doors with encrypted locks.*

"What should I have maintenance do to get the building ready for you?"

"Nothing. You should concentrate on getting the refinery back into production. Do not concern yourself with this building. The alterations I require will be done by a specialized concern that is a subsidiary of our parent company."

"I wasn't aware we had access to a company like that."

"They are in much demand, but my seniority allows me to preempt other divisions to have them work on my projects. They will finish the building to meet my requirements, including security. New cameras, re-enforced doors and jambs, as well as eight-digit locks on all entrances will fortify the building quite nicely. I will also have them upgrade security around the entire facility to military-grade standards. Please inform current staff they should not interfere with the work."

"Will do. Anything else you need to see? I can postpone a staff meeting that's supposed to start in thirty minutes."

"That will not be necessary. We can return to your building post haste."

"Yes, Boss."

Gunter suppressed a smile.

***

Chapter 11

Indiana State Police Post, Bristol, Indiana

"Ok, I need some volunteers."

Bill Hubbard groaned. "What for this time, Top?"

"Special detail. Head of the DEA pulled some strings to get us to deliver the two numbskulls from your traffic stop."

"All the way to Indianapolis?"

"No. I set up a transfer halfway in Wabash. By the way, thanks, it's nice of you and Taets to volunteer."

"Volun-told again," Trooper Hubbard said with a loud sigh. "We just finished a night shift, including typing up the reports from those two, Top."

"Seems to me it's day shift's problem now, First Sergeant," Taets chimed in.

"You would think. But Day Shift is stretched to the max with the propane depot disaster. Which means, you stopped 'em, you transport 'em, and get a couple hours overtime to boot. It'll help pay for that boat you're always talking about."

"Yeah, but I'm already bushed, and it'll take at least three hours. And that's if we don't run into any problems."

The First Sergeant offered a withering stare in response. "Put yourself in my shoes, Hubbard. I've got a major disaster on the Toll Road, and we are stretched thinner than mouse whiskers. Normally, I would let the perps sit here and rot, except right after talking to the DEA guy, I get a call from some bigwig in DC, followed by the governor himself. They would not give me a clue as to what is really going on, but I have a gut feeling I do not want to get in the middle of whatever it is. You know what they say about how it flows downhill. Long story short, I want the prisoners gone."

Taets sighed, and his shoulders slumped. "You're in the hot seat, so as usual, we'll back you. Remember, though, I'm supposed to have the next three days off to take the wife to the lake. We're going to spend some time together to fish and bring home a stringer full. Plan was to leave as soon as I finished the reports."

"So, you delay it for a few hours and get overtime to pay for bait."

"I don't want to sound like a whiner either," Hubbard said. "But the wife and I are going out for our anniversary. She will kill me if I'm not back in time. Plus, I'll need a little nap beforehand, so I don't fall asleep during the meal."

"Don't worry, you've got all the time in the world. You might even be back in time for lunch. Works out great for everybody when my two best guys step up. Doesn't get any better than that. So, without further ado, go get the old transport van ready and take off soon as you can. Brighton will get the info for you while I do the transfer paperwork."

"Who's driving, Bill?" TT asked as they stood and filed out of the briefing room.

"Does it matter? Like it or not, we're both going, Let's gas up and hit the road, though. Sooner we go, sooner we get back. I just need a minute to call the wife and let her know I might be a little late for dinner."

"Good idea. I'd better call my mine, too. Margie worries if I'm not home right after the shift. Said more than once she wishes I wasn't in law enforcement. But it's what I did in the service, and I happen to like it. Least I can do though, is keep her in the loop."

"Got to keep the home front happy," Bill replied.

"Or face the consequences."

They gassed up the marked state police transport van and loaded the suspects, after letting them use the bathroom. The prisoners were cuffed around the waist with a belly-chain and shackled at the ankles.

"They're not going anywhere in a hurry," Brighton remarked as he watched the process.

"Only if they go through us first," Hubbard replied.

Elkhart County Jail

"Well, that was a colossal dead end," Jake said to Uncle Bob as they drove across the street and parked behind another black Suburban with heavily tinted windows.

"State Police confiscated the rental truck, and they're holding it at their post in Bristol," Jake said to the agents milling around. "They also seized a small arsenal of weapons and a two-way radio. We need to get the radio and search the truck, so let's mount up."

Uncle Bob leaned over and asked in a low voice. "Your hand okay? You sure did a number on the hallway wall in the jail."

"I'm fine, just frustrated with the roadblocks we meet at every turn. Let's get to Bristol and see if we can sort through this mess."

Indiana State Route 15, South of Goshen

"How long do you figure this will take?" Taets asked. "I want to get to the lake before dark and catch a few fish for supper."

"What? We've been gone for fifteen minutes. It's another hour to Wabash."

"Should be fine, then. We'll be back by noon, two at the latest. Still can't believe we had to do this after being on duty all night. Glad I got that Big Gulp before we left. Mountain Dew can sure be your friend after a night shift. So, you said you're going out tonight?"

"Almost have to. Taking the wife out for our tenth anniversary. Even got the in-laws to babysit. I'm looking forward to it."

"You still celebrate anniversaries? We don't bother anymore."

"Your wife goes along with that?"

"Didn't say she didn't celebrate."

"Right. Hey, how about a quick bite after we drop these two off?"

"Best idea you've had lately. My stomach thinks my throat's been cut, and there's a mom-and-pop diner at the south end of town."

"You come down here often?"

"I spent most summers here on the farm with my mother's family. It gave my parents a break, although you know I was an angel, of course."

"Yeah, I could almost believe that…if I didn't know you," Bill could barely spit out the words as he laughed heartily.

"Would I lie about a thing like that?"

"You really want me to answer that?"

"No, probably not."

"So, what did you do down here?"

"My grandparents owned a pretty good-sized farm. Once we got old enough to work in the fields, we bailed hay, fed animals, and worked in the garden. We got to be kids once all the chores were done. Like, my cousin Dave and I used to shoot flies off the barn doors with our BB guns. And I got my first kiss behind that barn."

"With a girl?"

"No, with a cow. What do you think?"

"Sounds like a Norman Rockwell painting to me."

"Yeah, great memories. My aunt and uncle took over the place after my grandparents died. They still live there, although they lease the fields out. It isn't too far out of the way if you'd like to stop by and say hi."

"Been a long day, so maybe some other time."

"I hear that. You do anything like that as a kid?"

"Not the farm kid stuff. Dad was a city police officer who met my mom in the Auditor's Office in the County Building...."

Hubbard stopped in mid-sentence when a black SUV blasted past them. It rocked the prisoner van back and forth. "What an idiot. Good thing for him there's prisoners in back, or I'd pull him over in a heartbeat."

"Passing in a curve on a double-yellow line and speeding to boot. He sure needs to have the book thrown at him."

The SUV pulled up to within half a car length of a white Toyota Corolla.

Black SUV

Sasha pulled out to pass the small passenger car. "First, we make driver crash, then *politsiya* stop to help." He whipped the SUV hard to the right as it drew alongside the car. The small white Corolla swerved to miss the SUV and careened off the highway, bouncing and skidding sideways in the grass before crashing against a fence. "I move down road beyond curve where they cannot see and wait for *politsiya* to pull over."

"What if they do not stop?"

"They will. *Politsiya* here always stop to help innocents."

Indiana State Police Post, Bristol, Indiana

Jake and Bob strode into the brightly lit front lobby of the post and up to a counter with a hole set in a glass window. A bright-faced young State Policeman in a sharply creased uniform looked up from a computer terminal. "Can I help you gentlemen?"

"Yes, please. I'm Agent Jake Thomas, and this is Agent Bob Onkst. The Post Commander was told we were coming."

"We've been expecting you, sir It's not every day the Director of the NSA calls. I'll take you to the Post Commander, but...."

"Geez, I hate the "but" word."

"I'd better let the First Sergeant explain...."

"First Sergeant? We want the commander."

"Top is the commander. Left over from a restructuring the governor did back in the thirties. Modeled us like the military."

"Makes sense," Jake said as the man led them to the Post Commander's office.

A gray-haired man with crew-cut hair stood and offered a handshake. "Afraid I have bad news for you gentlemen. Somebody cut the lock on our impound yard and took the rental truck right out from under our noses. Footage shows two men in black clothing left with it just before dawn. We were getting a search warrant."

"Please tell me you have their radio?"

"Matter of fact, I do. Had it put in our evidence safe. I've been ordered to release it to you if you have a court order."

"From a federal judge, in fact. We need it for an ongoing investigation."

Top raised one eyebrow.

"Trust me," Jake said, "It's critical to national security."

The eyebrow went up further.

"Guess I'm digging myself in deeper, right? But take my word for it, we need that radio in the worst way."

"Don't suppose you can tell me why."

"Sorry, but the proof will be you won't hear anything in the media. Rest assured, you're helping stop some really bad guys from wreaking havoc on a lot of innocent civilians."

"That's good enough for me."

"No guard on the yard?"

"Only access is through the main gate, which is well lit and has cameras to boot. Otherwise, you go through the Post to get to the yard. It's got a twelve-foot chain-link fence topped with concertina wire. Thought we had pretty good security until this. Cameras did catch video of the two men who broke in."

"Let me guess from the look on your face, the images aren't all that clear."

The Post Commander sighed. "Night vision isn't great to begin with, and the perps apparently had experience at avoiding cameras. Odds are we won't catch anybody from the video."

"But you still have the radio?"

"Sure do. I had my evidence tech get it out of the vault and bring it up here so I could personally guard it...."

A young trooper rapped on the door frame. "Sorry to interrupt, Top, but you have a call on Line 2. Guy says it's an emergency."

"Thanks," the First Sergeant said as he punched the flashing light on his phone. He hung up a few tense minutes later. "The head of the DEA office just told me not to release the evidence to anybody but one of their agents. Said they had somebody en route as we spoke. Sorry, but he was very specific. Said nobody touches it but them."

Jake pulled a fax from his pocket. "Would you say an order from a federal judge trumps a voice on the phone?"

Top grinned. "Every day of the week, and twice on Sunday."

"If you wouldn't mind giving me the radio now, Top, I'd appreciate it. That way, if the DEA guy shows up, you can honestly say you no longer have it in your possession. You can even give him a copy of the court order to back you up."

"Sounds like a good idea," Top said as he spun the dial on a safe built into a credenza. "Here it is. What do I tell the DEA man if he asks who I gave it to?"

"Tell him you can't say, since it's a matter of...."

"National security, right?"

"You do catch on fast. Okay, then. Bob, get as much intel as you can from Top, and a copy of the video while I bring the Director up to date."

"Will do, Boss. Top, I need as much information on the truck and the men as possible. I'll also need copies of your reports, paperwork, and photos, if possible."

"Not a problem. Figured you'd want it, so it's right here." He pointed to a manilla folder on his desk. "The DEA guy will just have to pound sand. Didn't like the guy's attitude, anyway."

Bob interviewed the Post staff and called the tow truck driver while Jake contacted John Banner.

Jake and Bob were back in the First Sergeant's office twenty minutes later.

Top shook his head and grinned. "Don't know who you talked to, but the Governor called. He talked to the heads of the NSA and DEA on a conference call. Said there was a lot of shouting, but in the end, it came down to you getting the radio."

"Thanks, Top, we really appreciate your help." They shook hands, and Jake and

Bob left. "At least one of them knows what they're doing," Jake said.

Uncle Bob leaned against the hood of the command Suburban. "He runs a well-oiled machine. Troopers did a pretty good job documenting everything. Detailed notes with over a hundred photos. Seem to know their jobs."

Jake raised one eyebrow. "Other than the truck being stolen, right?"

"Well, there is that of course," Bob said as he examined the radio. "Battery level's low. Seems to work, but can't get anything on it. I guess the other radios are out of range."

"More than likely. Let's load up, team. We're burning daylight," Jake said.

***

Chapter 12

Indiana State Route 15, North of Wabash

"Holy cow, did you see that? They just ran that little car off the road." Bill slowed to get a better look at the scene. "Driver's getting out with her head bleeding. I'll call it in."

"Dispatch, 24-48."

"24-48, go ahead."

"Got a 10-50-PI. Black, full-size SUV with heavy tint just ran a white Toyota Corolla off the road and took off southbound. The SUV's license plate is obscured. Female vic in the Corolla is bleeding, so run an ambulance out to State Road 15 about two miles north of Wabash. Oh, and notify local PD."

"10-4, 24-48."

"Ok, TT, check her out."

Taets did not wait for the van to come to a full stop before he jumped out and adjusted his hat and duty belt out of habit. He slogged through mud and thick sawgrass. "Morning, Ma'am, I'm Trooper Taets. Are you ok?"

"I, uh, don't know. I hurt everywhere. Are my children okay?"

TT checked the backseat, "Yes, ma'am. Crying, but they appear to be unhurt. Good thing you had them in car seats. What is your name, and do you know what day it is?"

"What day? That's a strange question."

"Checking to see if you may have a concussion. I'd be worried if you didn't know your basic info. Not that I'm not concerned regardless."

"Yes, of course. Thank you, Officer. I'm Janice Whitley. Give me a second to check on the children." She opened the rear driver's side door and leaned in.

"How old are they?"

"Two, and four. They are my little angels. We just left from seeing their grandparents at the nursing home. We stop by every Tuesday to visit. It lifts my parent's spirits so much. Don't know what they'd do without the weekly visits."

"I've already called for an ambulance, but I need to get back to my partner and let him know what's going on. Be right back."

TT slogged back to the marked transport and opened the passenger door to talk to Hubbard, "Driver has minor bleeding from a small abrasion to her forehead, but seems to be okay otherwise. Well, other than pretty shaken up. Her two kids are in car seats in the back, and they're okay, too."

"That's good news...."

Both men looked up at the sound of an engine racing toward them. "Maybe some good Samaritan," Bill said. "Wait, that's the black SUV. What are they doing?" The SUV roared to a screeching halt a dozen feet from the front of the van.

"Go get men back," Sasha yelled at his crew. Three men leapt out with automatic weapons at the ready.

Both troopers drew their weapons, but it was too late. Countless searing rounds tore through the windshield and struck Bill Hubbard.

Terry Taets suffered the same fate as he stood next to the open passenger door. Rounds shattered his right arm and penetrated his chest. His face hit the pavement with a resounding thud, and he stared under the door at legs moving toward him. He tried to fire, but his hand would not work. Taets stared helplessly at the approaching attackers as his eyesight slowly faded to black.

"Get back doors open to free our men," Sasha yelled through the open window of the SUV. One of the men motioned for the prisoners to get down, smashed the window with the butt of his rifle, and opened the doors. Another mercenary unlocked the shackles of the two prisoners.

"*Politsiya* are dead?" Sasha asked as he sauntered up to the van.

"One is not. Wounded, but he maybe lives."

"Make him dead."

The mercenary fired several rounds into TT as he lay on the muddy ground, gurgling blood.

"What of woman and children?"

"*Bocc* says no witnesses, but children are too young to identify us. Let them live."

The terrified woman stood next to her car and screamed incoherently as one of Sasha's crew strolled toward her with a grim smirk.

Janice froze with fear. The young mother looked lovingly at her children for the last time. She turned back to the road and stared straight ahead. All expression faded from her face, and her arms dropped limply to her side.

The assailant moved to within an arm's length of the petrified woman and flipped a switch on the Uzi to make it semiautomatic. He placed the muzzle inches from her forehead.

Janice whimpered as she focused cross-eyed on the muzzle of the weapon. Her eyes widened, and she drew quick, ragged breaths. Her knees sagged, and a yellow stream ran down her leg. She tried to scream, but no sound came out.

The man stared at the helpless woman for a moment and pulled the trigger. The back of her head exploded, and she looked like a ragdoll as her body went limp. Her lifeless body fell to the ground with mouth open and eyes vacant.

The thug watched as her face slowly turned ashen. The only sounds were the breeze blowing through tall grass and trees, and the calls of cicadas. The frightened cries of the children turned to whimpers as he strode back to the prisoner transport van.

Sasha said to the other men, "Other team should have truck back from *politsiya*, so we must leave. *Bocc* says to take US-24 east to Fort Wayne, then north to Toledo, Ohio."

"Why do we go there?" one of the gunmen asked.

"Because *Bocc* says so. Leave questions to me and *Bocc*. You ask too many things. Do you write book?"

The man shrugged his shoulders and walked in silence to the black SUV. The smell of cordite hung heavy in the air, and broken bodies lay scattered about.

Children's mournful screams once again broke the tranquility of the grassy meadow. The only other sound was spent brass crunching under tactical boots.

How do I report to Consortium with so many witnesses? Sasha thought as he dialed the sat phone. "*Bocc*, we have rescued men with no casualties. We will soon join you."

"You have recovered my equipment?"

"No, *politsiya* have radio and weapons."

"Do men tell *politsiya* anything?"

"No, *Bocc*. They say *politsiya* did not torture them, so they say nothing."

"Very good. Witnesses?"

"No, *Bocc*, Troopers are dead. A woman witness is dead also."

"Is too bad for her. You will meet me at location I give to you. I shall be there in two hours. We stay for three days, then continue mission."

"Yes, *Bocc*. Map says we are two-and-one-half-hours from you. We must refuel and eat, so maybe three hours."

"Good. Keep my men in van, no matter what. Bring food to them. I do not wish for them to be seen, especially by *politsiya*."

"Yes, *Bocc*, is understood." Sasha ended the call and put the sat phone on the center console.

"Scenery is better in Russia," a man in the backseat said. "I am tired of cornfields and cows."

Sasha smiled. "Yes, but in Russia *politsiya* and military are everywhere. We could not simply drive away. In America we are free to do so. What a country. We will stop to get food when we are away from this place."

"Is good, for I am hungry. I want smorgasbord, what here is called buffet."

"I would also like that." *I will call mother when we stop. Men will be distracted with eating and using facilities.*

171

Airstrip Outside Hagerstown, Maryland

"Let's see, should I call you Justin, or Glenn?" Jack posed the mostly rhetorical question to Justin Todd. "By the way, you're welcome for your new accommodations. They should suit you for now. Not as nice as your big fancy RV, but that monster would be easy to track. Plus, moving it from the storage unit might raise some flags. I found a place just rotting away a year or so ago and snapped it up for a song. Did some work on the inside but left the outside looking like it's about to crumble. You'll also welcome the upgrades to the bathroom. I know I do."

"Justin."

"I'm sorry, what? Oh, you want to be called Justin? Good, it's easier for me since that's how I knew you when you were Executive Assistant to the NSA Director."

"If I may ask, what are your plans regarding me?"

"Wow, you really do talk that way, even when not undercover. All righty then, let me lay it out for you. I'm going to hire you and send you back to work for the NSA. What do you think of that?"

"If you desire my opinion, that may prove to be nearly impossible. Although, with your seemingly endless resources, I suppose you might accomplish it. I would anticipate some potential difficulties, but I could skillfully deal with any problems."

"Good. By the way, you can drop the hoity-toity act. I know you went to college for a measly year and a half. The Consortium spent a ton of money on your backstory, but I found the truth."

"You must admit, sir, being well-spoken has its advantages. I used my demeanor to obtain the position in the office of the Director and gained his confidence. I see some benefit in your proposal and assume you will not harm me if I am of value to you."

"Oh, really? Think you'd have me by the short hairs? Well, I can always change my mind." He put the muzzle of a 1911 to Justin's forehead. "After all, I've been known to go off the rails now and then. Besides, I have another iron in the fire. Where do you think I got your name?"

Justin's blank stare indicated he had no clue.

"Remember, the Consortium is still after you. I can let them have you and take what you stashed away. How would anybody know?" Jack leaned back and slowly lowered the pistol to his lap. "Think about it. You could come out of this smelling like a rose. Work for me, get your cushy NSA position back, and work for the Consortium, too. You get to double-dip, and I'll even let you keep the luxury RV. I have big plans for you, and you can make a butt-load of money in the process."

"I imagine having three bosses could be the sort of challenge I crave. How much, exactly, would a butt-load of money be?"

Jack laughed, "Let's just say it would take a month of Sundays to count it. I pay my people good money when they make my dealings with others easy and profitable. The more I make, the more you make. As long as you are loyal to me, it's that simple."

"Precisely how will you return me to my former position?"

"I have a plant inside the NSA who will take the fall for you. He's in a strategic position, and his takedown will take the heat off you. Clues have been placed to lead right to him. It's like when a single rock is kicked away that eventually leads to a landslide."

"Yes, but you must be aware Banner, and the Consortium will thoroughly investigate before allowing my return."

"A polygraph will undoubtedly be done by both organizations. All you need to do is tell a select part of the truth that I help you craft. A little help from drugs that are undetectable, and you won't fail because it's the truth, minus a detail or two."

"The NSA is competent at rooting out this sort of thing."

"So you would think. They think they can trust people because they vet them so often. What they don't realize is investigators can be pointed down the wrong path time and time again. Unless, that is, something jumps up and slaps them. The Consortium, on the other hand, tends to make problem employees simply disappear. I can point them away from you, so they look at you as a victim, not a threat. It'll work."

Justin stared intently at Morgan. "How do I know you are the real thing and not

some impos...."

Morgan jerked the 1911 from his lap and fired a round that blew within a hair's breadth of Justin's ear. "What'd they tell you about my temper?"

"That you have a short fuse, sir." Justin's head swayed back and forth, and a loud ringing in his ears made it difficult to hear. He made out a few words by reading Jack's lips and facial expression.

"…more proof?"

"No, sir, I believe you have made your point quite clear."

"Good, now back to business."

Justin stuck a finger in his ear and wiggled it to try to clear the ringing as he concentrated on the madman sitting across from him. *I will survive. I will survive.*

***

Chapter 12

Indiana State Police Post

Brighton dropped the front desk phone and ran to the commander's office.

The First Sergeant glanced up at the ashen expression on his young charge. "What is it, Brighton? What's wrong?"

The young trooper fought back tears. "Got a call from Wabash PD. Somebody ambushed our transport van on State Road 15."

Top shot out of his seat. "That can't be right. I sent two of my best men. Nobody could sneak up on them. It's not possible."

"Apparently it was, Top. Both are dead, and the perps are long gone. A young mother was run off the road during the incident and is dead, too. Her two babies were alive in the car. First the propane disaster, and now this. What in the world is going on, Top?"

"Who knows? But I have a gut feeling the two are somehow connected."

"I know we're stretched to the max. Should I call Breman Post to see if they have anybody available? They're closer than us."

"Good thinking, Brighton, but no. We need to step aside and let somebody else investigate since our men were victims. Wabash doesn't have the manpower to investigate an attack like this. I'll call Indianapolis to see how they want to handle it."

The First Sergeant exhaled sharply and sank into his chair as the magnitude of the disaster struck him. "First the propane depot, and now this. They've got to be connected. I need to notify Hubbard and Taets's widows in person. But first, get that point of contact from the NSA on the phone.

I bet they know more than they're letting on. I want to know what they're holding back."

Truck Stop On I-69, Fort Wayne, Indiana

"Morgan, is Sasha."

"Sasha, my old friend. How are you this fine afternoon?"

"You are not friend. I owe debt to you, so I cooperate. We get men back from State Troopers and leave no witnesses. We stop in Fort Wayne, Indiana for food and gas. Others think I call Yancy to report progress."

"So where are you headed now?"

"Warehouse in Port of Toledo. Yancy is to soon be there with devices. But I, myself, will not be there for several hours."

"Tell me all the particulars about your trip, and the warehouse in the marina. I also need details on what's in the trucks we talked about last time."

Sasha shifted further behind a truck in the parking lot to help conceal him. "I do not like this. I feel like traitor."

"The money I'm paying you should help you get over that. Now give me every bit of information you have."

A wealth of information was exchanged in the remaining minutes of the call.

GoldStar Refinery

The golf cart pulled away from the curb and had only gone a hundred yards when an agitated man ran onto the path, forcing Jim to slam on the brakes. He stopped just short of a pot-bellied man dressed in tight overalls sporting various stains and unzipped halfway down his chest.

"I wanna talk to you, you no good SOB," the middle-aged man shouted and pointed at Jim.

Gunter sat quietly with his hands folded in his lap after unsnapping the shoulder holster under his jacket.

"What seems to be the problem, Harry?" Jim said in a calm voice.

"You, that's what. We worked oil fields together for almost thirty years. So, tell me why I just checked the shift schedule, and I ain't on it."

"You did it to yourself. I made it clear the last time you got into a shoving match that you'd be suspended for two weeks. You can't bully the rest of the crew when you don't get your way. I watched the video from yesterday, and it looks like that's exactly what you did with one of the new guys."

"Useless piece of rat turd. If I told him once, I told him a hundred times not to...."

"A hundred times, huh? I don't see where you ever wrote him up once."

"Wrote him up? Shouldn't have to. I tell him to jump, he's supposed to ask how high, and how far."

"We've talked about this more than once. You're not on a rig anymore. This is a refinery that operates under different rules."

"Well, maybe I don't think much of your stupid-ass rules," the red-faced Harry spit out the words like a machine gun.

"Which is why I'm suspending you. Hopefully, you'll think over your situation and come to your senses during the two weeks. Catch up on some home repairs, go fishing, or do something useful that gets your mind back on track."

"Or maybe I'll just whip your sorry broke-ass butt right here and now."

"You wouldn't be the first man who tried and lost. It's up to you," Jim said as he slowly slid from the seat and rose to his full six-foot-five inches. "On the other hand, keep in mind I don't take kindly to threats from anyone, especially one of my crew. So tread carefully before you decide what you're going to do. Better yet, go home and cool off. Or would you rather I throw you out the front gate with a pink slip stapled to your forehead?"

The color drained from Harry's face, and he looked down at the gravel. "Pink slip? Fire me? You can't do that. I got two kids in college. I need this job."

"I know, but you also need to follow the rules, especially when they're clear-cut and in writing. Do both of us a favor and go home. I'll see you back here in two weeks if you're so inclined. I just can't have you setting a bad example for the new guys."

"Bad example? What the hell are you saying, Jim? We go back a long way. Ain't never known you to be such a tight ass."

"Times change, Harry, and we have to change with them. Also, it's Mister Ballard when we're on the job. And remember, it's my way, or the highway. You understand what I'm saying?"

Harry stammered as he replied, "Uh, yes, sir, Mister Ballard. Don't know what got into me, and thanks for not firing me on the spot. I truly am grateful."

"No problem. You're one of my best men when you pay attention. Besides, we all need to blow off a little steam now and then. Long as we don't let it get out of hand."

"Yes, sir. I'll just go punch out now, and maybe take that suggestion about fishing. Could do me some good. See you in two weeks with my head on straight."

Jim returned to the golf cart. "Sorry that happened."

"Not at all, Jim. You handled the situation quite well. I am impressed with your management style."

"Thanks. It's just another part of the job."

Ohio Turnpike

"Move to right lane for exit," Yancy spoke into the radio. At I-75 we go north. We refuel in twenty minutes."

"Where do we go later, *Bocc*?" Vasily asked.

"Do not ask stupid question on radio where others may hear. Do you understand I lead, and you follow?" Yancy spit into the mic. "Sasha, do you have inventory of what I lose to *politsiya*?"

"*Da, Bocc,* as you order."

"Is good. Vasily, you will inspect cargo when we stop to ensure is safe and secure."

Yancy's guttural voice burst from the radio as they drove onto the pier in Toledo, "Man at warehouse ahead on right will open door so we may pull into building. I do not wish for others to see us. Alexi, have two men hide at each end to secure perimeter. They must report everything they see, no matter how small."

"*Da, Bocc.*"

"We will be here for two, maybe three days. Like usual, get food from different restaurants."

"Yes, *Bocc*. Do we have second location, like Chicago?"

"No, for we will not be here long."

Pay Phone Outside Warehouse in Toledo

"Mother, it has been two days since we talked last. How is dear Uncle Maxim?"

"Oh, Sasha, Doctor sends him to hospital. Maxim is in ICU, and I worry he may not survive."

"Will he be there two or three days?"

"Doctors do not say. You must call tomorrow, if possible."

"I will try. We are in Toledo, Ohio in warehouse near wharf to we wait for ship *S.P. Lee* to pick up cargo. Then we travel by truck to New York City and Washington, DC. Are you okay, mother?"

"Yes, God watches over me. Do you eat enough?"

"I try. Life is hard, but we suffer now for better life. Give my love to family."

"I will. Be safe, my beloved son."

Sasha hung up the pay phone, stuffed his hands into the pockets of the overcoat and walked toward the warehouse. His head was down, but he searched for anybody who might be watching.

GoldStar Refinery

Gunter listened as the side door of the R&D building closed and locked behind him with a steel thunk. He walked across the covered parking lot to where Jim Ballard waited under a three-sided metal shelter.

"Good morning, Mister Ballard."

Ballard sat on the golf cart smoking one of his trademark stogies and watched a ring of smoke drift up toward the metal roof. "Three months have gone on by, and you still call me Mister Ballard. What's it gonna take to get you to call me Jim?"

"I, uh, um, will endeavor to do so henceforth."

Jim nodded and held the cigar up. "This is one of the few places on site I can do this, since the rest of the complex is off-limits to smoking. Welcome to the NRF," he said with a chuckle.

"NRF?"

"Nicotine Recovery Facility. It's an inside joke, and another name for the smoking pen. Would you like one?"

"I assume it is from your personal humidor?"

"Sure is. Brought them with me from the Angry Leprechaun. I usually keep at least one in my saddlebag in a sealed metal case and today I threw in an extra for you. Most people don't understand the quality of a premium cigar. On the other hand, I figured you might appreciate the delicacy and rich flavor." Jim handed Gunter a cigar and the cutter.

Gunter cut off the end, lit it, and took a long draw. "This is indeed one for a discerning palate. May I ask where you acquired it?"

"My wife and I went to Honduras last summer to visit her brother, Guillermo. He's friends with Pierre Lafayette, the owner of a tobacco plantation. I introduced Pierre to a very fine Irish Whiskey, and he named a new cigar line after me."

"A line of cigars named after you. That is quite impressive."

"Serendipity. I just happened to visit on a good day."

"With the right gift and a friendly attitude. Am I correct?"

"Guess that might could have been a big part of it." Jim leaned back with his hands behind his head and grinned.

Gunter followed Jim's lead as they avoided the hot Texas sun in the shade of the awning. Gunter smiled. "You were right, the delicate fragrance and taste of the cigar is a pleasure."

Jim spoke after a while, "I see your crew has done extensive work to the operations building. Does it meet your expectations?"

"It is not perfect, yet. There are a few final touches, but it will suffice."

"Also, couldn't help but notice the huge air-handlers you put in. The sweltering Texas heat getting to you?"

"I must admit I am more accustomed to the higher latitudes where heat like this is rare."

"As you'll hear often down here, it's not the heat, it's the humidity."

"I believe that to be true. Shall we continue with our tour to assess progress? How are we doing, vis-à-vis the timeline I set out?"

"Right on time, for the most part. There was a problem with the intake lines from the marine park. I figured crude might have settled in the pipes, and I was right. But flushing the lines solved the problem. We're back in business and only a little behind schedule."

"Understandable. However, I expect to adhere to the plan as closely as possible."

"No problem, Gunter. I built delays into the timeline for things like this. Pumps are in good repair and won't need to be rebuilt. Lines have been pressure tested to 50 percent over and held, so I don't see it holding us up more than a day or two, at the most."

"Good. As you are aware, delays have consequences."

"Not sure what that means, and maybe I don't want to know." Jim took another puff and stared into the distance.

***

Chapter 13

Gunter's Office

"Good afternoon, Commissioner," Gunter spoke into the satellite phone. "I am pleased to report the reactivation of the refinery proceeds on schedule. I have established a rapport with Ballard and find him to be quite capable."

"Excellent work, Mister Wilhelm. Then I, too am pleased. I assume you have an estimated time of completion, yes?"

"I am still assessing the situation and calculating the timeline to begin processing crude. I will furnish you with a detailed report as soon as possible, perhaps as early as tomorrow."

"Very good, Wilhelm, I knew I could rely on you, despite recent difficulties. This is a project that is vital to our global interests. I look forward to supplying our clients with the critical products they require, and in return, they will come to depend on us for favorable pricing and stability. Over time, an understanding of what support we require from them will emerge. We shall establish a firm foot-hold in strategic locations around the world."

"Your vision of world order is admirable, Commissioner." *Even though most of it probably came from subordinates.*

"Indeed. I must now return to other business." He disconnected the call and pressed the intercom button. "Send in the masseuse."

Dockside Warehouse, Toledo, Ohio

"Vasily, boat will be here tomorrow afternoon," Yancy told his lieutenant. "Lead-lined containers wait for us at office. Take two men to retrieve them and return to warehouse so we may pack tonight. When do you last check perimeter?"

"One-half hour. *Politsiya* come by last night, drive around buildings, but do not leave car. Such lax simpletons would be sent to *gulag* in Russia. I like lazy American *politsiya* who make our work easy. Not like troopers on highway."

"Is unfortunate troopers interfered," Yancy replied. "But is good they take nothing to stop mission. Is good we do not shoot at *politsiya*. We would win, of course, but BlackStar force would be on us in minutes. Is better to live to fight another day."

Vasily cleared his throat and shuffled his feet. "Uh, *Bocc,* I have something difficult I must discuss with you."

"Tell me as we go upstairs to office."

Vasily closed the door behind him. "We may have problem with Sasha."

"What is problem?"

"Boris brings back food and sees Sasha on pay phone."

"Who does he talk to?"

"He talks very softly, but Boris hears 'mother' twice. Also 'uncle in hospital'."

"Check to see if Sasha has family in hospital. I must know today if he is danger to mission."

Gunter Wilhelm's Refinery Office

"There is no need for your smug look," Gunter said to the blond-haired, blue-eyed man sitting across the desk. "We are both aware you are here to babysit me."

Jaeger Muller shifted uncomfortably in the armchair, and it wobbled. Gunter chose the chair for just that quality to literally unbalance the Consortium snitch.

"Not at all, sir. I am here to lend whatever assistance you may require, and I thank you for being so forthright."

"I thought it only fair for us to be honest with each other. My staff are quite capable, so it would seem your sole purpose is to report back to the Commissioner. However, before you do, allow me to mention I am available to clarify any concerns before you do so."

"I will keep that it in mind. I detect a slight Austrian accent. Is that your origin?"

"My personal background is none of your business. Limit your concern to our working relationship."

Jaeger was visibly set back but recovered in an instant. "I apologize if I offended you, sir. I was trying to establish a rapport. With your permission, I will return to my office."

"You did not cause undue offense, and yes, your office may be the best place for you. Feel free to spend as much time as you like there."

Gunter rose to signal the conclusion of the meeting. Jaeger took the hint and followed him to the door.

"And yes, you are correct. Part of my childhood was spent in Austria, and I would say your accent indicates familiarity with Bavaria, yes?"

Jaeger's eyebrows rose slightly. "How very perceptive of you, sir" he said as he stepped through the door.

"It comes from a lifetime of assessing people," Gunter said as he closed the door.

Dockside Warehouse, Toledo, Ohio

"Vasily, you will supervise men to load nuclear device into one lead-lined container. Be sure is watertight and use much padding in case container falls."

"Should we also pack other bomb in second container?"

"Yes, but you must leave room for extra items."

"Bigger crate goes on ship?"

"Yes, but you must be careful. One misstep and many people die. Damage weapons and you suffer slow, agonizing death."

"Do we seal crates?"

"Seal small container we take with us. Hide alarm device underneath container that goes on ship but do not activate. Put lid on, but do not lock. I will do so later."

Two hours later Yancy motioned Vasily over to him. "Boat has arrived. Choose four men and come with me to dock. Be ready for treachery. Is common."

"Boat belongs to Consortium, yet you expect trouble?"

"No, but we must always be ready."

The climb up the steep boarding ramp ten minutes later left Vasily breathless. Yancy was in the lead and said over his shoulder, "Physical fitness is important to our job."

"Maybe more exercise is good."

"Is good we do not carry crates up this way. Hoist in middle of ship will do so."

"For that I am happy," Vasily replied.

"You are Captain of this boat?" Yancy said to a man in his fifties with salt and pepper hair and a ruddy, weathered face.

"Yes, but technically, is ship."

Yancy scowled as he recited the pass code, "Bees sting."

"But pollinate flowers and crops."

The captain smiled and extended his hand. "I am Pavel Gorsky, Mister Yancy, The Consortium sends regards."

"You must call me Gregori."

"And I would be pleased if you call me Pavel when others are not around. I am ready to load cargo, but first we share vodka." He gestured behind him to a table and chairs.

Yancy nodded to Vasily, who joined him, while the Andy, the First Mate sat on the other side with Gorsky.

Gorsky poured water glasses nearly full with the potent liquor and said, *Ваше здоровье*."

"To your health as well, Captain," Yancy replied as he raised his glass. "I do not wish to be rude, but we both have tight schedule. I wish to load crates soon and continue to my destination."

"*Da*, I deliver your crates to Antwerp. What do you require from me?"

"Crates should go in cargo hold at bottom. Do you have other cargo?"

"None. Consortium says only yours."

"Is good. Is military ship?"

"Yes. Keel was laid in 1966 and launched in 1967. Was delivered to US

Navy as survey ship in 1968. Two-hundred feet long, with beam of thirty-nine feet. Displaces thirteen-hundred metric tons of water with draft of only fourteen feet. Used for US Navy research until university acquired for civilian research programs. Declared excess five years ago. Purchased by our mutual friends at surplus auction."

"A wise move, to be sure. Why does Consortium send large ship for one crate?"

Gorsky switched to Russian, "To cross ocean is better to be too big, not too small. Cargo must be important to them."

"*Da*, very valuable. It must be safe."

"You have my word. But I can do nothing if Coast Guard boards ship."

"Then you must be careful.'

"Age of ship will help. Patches on cargo hold walls hide many compartments. Your crate will not be found."

"Good. Now for other conditions."

"Conditions? Order says transport crate to Antwerp. Nothing more."

"I send two men to guard crate."

"Orders say nothing of this."

"I pay large sum if you do exactly as I say," Yancy said with a grim smile.

"You have no authority to dictate orders to me," Gorsky roared as he stood and leaned over the table.

Yancy stared at his watch. "Message should be with radio officer. He will confirm change in orders. I will wait," Yancy said in Russian. He stared at a clueless Andy, who watched his captain storm away.

Gorsky returned a few minutes later and took note of Yancy's calm demeanor. "I think there must be more to your request...."

"Is not request...is order. You will receive substantial bonus for trip from me to guarantee you and crew remain silent to everybody."

"How much bonus?"

"Two million American dollars for you, fifty thousand for First Mate, Radio Officer and helmsmen. Rest of crew receive ten thousand. Is adequate?"

"B…but, of course. I am not accustomed to such generosity."

"Consortium does not pay well?"

"Yes, but additional bonus for one trip is unusual. What do you demand in return?"

"Follow orders and maintain contact with me." Yancy handed Gorsky a satellite phone.

"What are other requirements?"

"Allow my men unrestricted access."

"Other than living quarters?"

"They are discreet. Will knock first."

"Is unusual, but I will allow, except for my personal cabin."

"Good. Give keys to them when they come on ship. Vasily will supervise loading of crate while I observe."

Gorsky shrugged his shoulders. "Mister McDonough, please take Vasily with you to direct deck crew."

"Aye, aye, Cap'n," Andy said as he stood. He turned to Vasily. "How big is this crate, and are there any special requirements I should know about since it's going onto my ship?"

"I thought was his ship?"

"As First Mate, I serve as Captain if anything happens to him."

"Let us hope nothing does," Vasily replied with a smirk.

"Whatever. Again, any special requirements?"

"Only must be hidden and secure."

"Our crew is used to that. It will be locked down tight and out of sight. How big is it?"

"Is twelve-feet long by six-feet wide, and five-feet tall."

"Any hazardous material?"

"Not for you to worry."

"I am responsible for the safety of this ship and crew. That includes making sure cargo doesn't send us to Davey Jones's locker. Maybe I need to open it to be sure."

Yancy glanced at Gorsky. "No one must open crate. I tell you is fine."

Gorsky stared at Yancy for a moment. "Consortium ships often carry cargo with no clue of contents. Mister McDonough only wishes to protect ship. But Consortium would not allow material that might endanger ship, so continue with loading."

"Aye, aye, Captain."

The onboard crane slowly positioned the crate over the open cargo hold. "Easy, let down slowly," Vasily said into the radio.

"This ain't my first rodeo," the crane operator responded. "Let me do my job."

Andy leaned over and said to Vasily, "He's been doing this for over twenty years. Never seen him drop anything."

Vasily offered a steely stare in reply. "Like you, I do my job."

"Sure, and for your information, I'm a hawsepiper."

"What is this hawsepiper?"

"A man who worked his way up through the ranks. I've spent time from stem to stern, bilge to bridge, and I know my job."

Vasily spoke into the radio, "Captain, do you see crate come down?"

"Yes, Vasily. Mister Yancy and I are at false wall where crate is to be stored. Spot welds and old paint scrapings are mixed in with fresh paint. No one will know wall is not single piece of steel."

"How long to depart, Pavel?" Yancy asked.

Gorsky rubbed his chin. "Not today. Additional stores must be ordered for your men. Sometime in next three days."

"I prefer today or tomorrow at latest. Your men can move about ship but must report to my men if they leave dock."

"I control my crew...."

"Yes, but now we are partners. I can take crate and demand refund, but you would be forced to tell *Bocces* why you refuse cargo."

"Consortium will not return your funds. For you must know this, yes?"

"Then you must make plans to leave soon with my cargo. I will return tomorrow."

T.c. Miller and J.A. Schrock

***

Chapter 14

Dockside Warehouse

Vasily sat across the desk from Yancy. "I get information about Sasha."

"Good. He is traitor, yes?"

"Is possible, but I think maybe not. Hospital in New York says there is patient Maxim in ICU. Nurse says older woman visits Maxim daily. Could be mother of Sasha."

"Sasha knows rules, but if my family is in hospital, I, too, will call. I do not like this, but do not punish him. Have men load crate in truck. We leave after I visit Gorsky one last time."

"*Da, Bocc*, as you wish."

"Very good. You impress me, but do not get big head. You must prove yourself."

Dockside Aboard the *SP Lee*

"Everything is in order, Mister Yancy."

"Good, Captain. Here is money for supplies. What is schedule for ship?"

"Three days through Great Lakes...."

"Why so long?"

"Sailing and lockage time...."

"What is lockage time?"

"Locks adjust level of water from one place to next. Is necessary to avoid rapids and circumvent dams."

"This I did not know."

Gorsky continued, "Nine days sailing to Antwerp, one day for Customs inspection, and one day to unload."

"Loading crate takes only one hour."

"Union rules in Belgium are strict."

"Can you not pay bribe?"

"Cargo would be seized if caught."

Yancy looked at Gorsky with distrust, cleared his throat and said, "Would be very bad for them...and you. Arrangements are made for transport of cargo to Switzerland?"

"Yes, and forged papers for your men so they may travel with cargo."

"Is pleasure doing business with man who knows how to do these things."

"Only takes much money."

"But is necessary, yes?" *Is small amount compared to nine hundred million US dollars I have in secret accounts.*

"Money greases the machinery of commerce," Gorsky replied.

"I do not mind if it greases the palms of those who help me." *It will not be long before I have ten times more, and control of the Consortium.*

"Commissioner will be pleased to receive crate, yes?"

"But of course." *It would be nice to see reaction of Commissioner when cargo arrives, but I would not want to be within one hundred kilometers a day later..* "I will call you on sat phone each day at noon. When do you leave here?"

"Very soon."

"Take good care of my shipment or suffer consequences."

Gorsky locked eyes with Yancy before replying, "As always."

They shook hands and Yancy walked down the gangplank to a waiting Vasily.

"Men have sat phones and code words, yes?"

"*Da, Bocc.*"

The ship's crew pulled the heavy ropes that tied the ship in place aboard and stowed them for the ocean voyage.

Yancy and his men watched as the ship sailed out of sight. It would soon transition from Maumee Bay to Lake Erie and proceed through the St. Lawrence Seaway to the Atlantic Ocean.

Dockside Warehouse, Toledo Ohio

"Men are ready to leave?" Yancy asked.

"*Da, Bocc,* Vasily replied. "Trucks are packed and fueled. Men wait for you to speak to them."

"Are they formed as two teams?"

"As you order. First team of truck and two SUV's with small crate for you. Second crew has two trucks and two SUVs."

"You will supervise second crew. You have route and address, yes?"

"I memorize route and code words."

"You memorize timeline too?"

"*Da, Bocc.* I can write backward."

"Is good. Stay with plan and we will succeed. Remember, men often fail because of simple mistake."

"Trust me, I will not fail you."

Yancy inhaled deeply and coughed. "I will not miss damp, stale air with smell of waste oil and rotted fish."

"We go in fifteen minutes," Igor yelled at Joanna as he pounded on the side of the shipping container. The heavy metal latch of the door squeaked, clanked, and dropped into the unlocked position a minute later.

"Do not throw waste on me, and I will not kill you."

"I won't, but don't handcuff me so tight this time."

Igor leaned back and laughed. "Oh, but I must. I do not wish to explain to *Bocc* if you escape. He might kill me with bare hands."

"I promise I won't try anything, but last time left marks, and cut off circulation."

"You will not have circulation if *Bocc* does not need you. Lay on belly, arms to side, and turn head away from me."

Joanna obeyed.

Igor knelt cautiously next to her, firmly grasped her wrist, and locked one side of the handcuffs. He spun her until her feet were away from him. A quick move across her back brought the other arm to him and he fastened her wrists together. "Is not too bad?"

"Thank you," she replied. *At least I left enough DNA to show I was here.* She took a deep breath. *Got to maintain a positive mental attitude. Find me, Jake!*

"Hood is next. I will help you sit up."

"My God, don't you ever wash this thing? Between sweat, drool, and whatever that other smell is, it's disgusting."

Igor grinned. "I never wear it. As Americans say, it sucks to be you." He dropped the hood over her head and tied it.

Kelly's Bar and Tavern, Brooklyn, NY

"Let's cut to the chase, Maury," Jack Morgan said impatiently. "As leasing manager for the Consortium in New York, you know where Gregori Yancy and his crew will soon be. So where do I find them?"

"You know I can't tell you that. They'd have my butt in a sling in a New York minute."

"Which is funny, considering that's where we are. But that would be only if they found out, which they won't. You'll just have to decide whose bad side you want to be on, mine or theirs. Keeping in mind, of course, I live in this country, and they don't."

"Yeah, yeah, sure, but they got enforcers all over the place."

"So do I, but that's beside the point. I've got the Director of North American Operations in my back pocket. I can protect you, but who will protect you from me? Don't bother trying to figure it out. I'll tell you. Nobody, that's who. On the other hand, play ball with me and you'll find out I pay great bonuses."

"How great?"

"What would it take? Nobody will ever know where I get my information."

"I don't know...something in the neighborhood of ten thousand, maybe?"

"I gotta tell you, Maury, you must be hanging out in some pretty cheap neighborhoods. Personally, I like neighborhoods in the fifty grand range. How would that suit you?"

"Yeah, I think you got my attention."

"And there would be a lot more to follow. So, do we have a deal?"

"Maybe I should sleep on it."

"You could, but you should know I have copies of the books you're using to skim money from the Consortium. I'm sure you know what they do to embezzlers isn't pretty."

"Wait, hold on a second there. Marty's the only one who's got those, and he ain't gonna rat me out. We been friends since grade school."

"You know, he probably wouldn't. Well, except when the money's right, and when you consider the lewd photos I have of him. So, he agreed to help me."

Maury gave Morgan a sad look of resignation. "You gotta be kidding me. All right, tell me exactly what I gotta do to make this go away."

"Not a whole lot. Just give me the address of the place you leased to Yancy."

"Ain't nobody ever gonna find out where you got it?"

"I'm a man of my word, and in this business, that's worth a ton."

"You got the cash on you?"

Jack nodded to Wild Bill. "Give it to him."

Wild Bill extended a briefcase but held on to it after Maury grasped the handle. He moved within a foot of the smaller man and leaned down. "You throw my boss over a cliff, and I guarantee what the Consortium might do to you ain't nothin' compared to what I'll do. Your new address will have pain written all over it right before the first shovel of dirt hits your face and all you can breathe is dust. Got it?"

"Yeah, I got it."

New York City

"Bocc, is Vasily. I am in city where you order me to go. Warehouse is thirty minutes from here," Vasily spoke in a low tone into the encrypted satellite phone.

"Is good, Vasily, as I also am near to destination in other city. Do you remember plan?"

"Da, Bocc. I call contact when we finish and use passwords like you say. Contact will take us to warehouse. We wait like timeline says and finish plan." Vasily glanced around the SUV for a tail.

"Good job, Vasily," Yancy hit the end button on the satellite phone and stared out the window at nothing in particular, as a DC Metro train sped by in the opposite direction. He sighed, took a long draw from a cigar, and settled into the seat of the SUV.

Gunter Wilhelm's Refinery Office

The phone jarred Gunter out of an accounting review of Consortium North American operations for the previous week.

"Mister Wilhelm, I trust you are doing well, and hope the project is proceeding at a good pace?"

"Yes, Commissioner, I am well, as I hope you are. I assume you have my latest report on the refinery?" Gunter swiveled the chrome and leather executive chair to gaze out heavily tinted windows at the bay.

"Yes, indeed, Wilhelm. I have reviewed them, and it would appear the refinery project is on schedule to soon produce matériel for our customers. Have you encountered any problems?"

"Only the expected, and they are manageable. The workforce is different from that to which I am accustomed, but adjustments have been made."

"Good. Your latest report shows your office building is nearing completion. How soon will you be fully operational?"

"The final touches will be made within a week or so, pending arrival of the shipment...."

"Shipment?"

"Uh, yes, Commissioner. You informed me last week of a shipment of computers."

"I did? Let me check."

Gunter heard faint conversation despite the Commissioner putting his hand over the phone, although most of it was unintelligible.

"Yes, yes, Wilhelm, I now recall our conversation. The computers are indeed en route and should arrive at your location in less than a week."

"I understand how it could slip your mind with the complexity of Consortium operations...."

"Are you inferring that I might be incapable of managing more than one project?"

"No, no, of course not. I was only attempting to commiserate with you."

"Are you indeed? I grow increasingly weary of those who question my ability to perform my duties."

"I would never do that, sir. Serving you and the Consortium is my sole intention. Please allow me to continue my assessment. The arrival and installation of the computers will allow me to devote more time to revenue generating operations. That includes the production of petroleum products. Operation of the facility at full capacity should begin shortly."

Gunter poured ice water from a cut-glass carafe into a crystal tumbler and settled back into his chair. "I will supervise the installation...."

"Before you continue, Gunter, allow me to inform you of something. I have other matters I wish to discuss, but not even on a secure device. The Executive Committee has moved the quarterly board meeting forward to next week. Have Jaeger take over the refinery project whilst you attend. My secretary will arrange a flight for you, and I shall see you then."

"As you wish, Commissioner, but what shall I do about the shipment of computers?"

"Jaeger can supervise their installation."

Over my dead body. "If you insist, although I am more eminently qualified. Still, I will defer to your judgment. How long will I be in Leipzig?"

"That has not yet been determined, but you should plan for a week."

The call was terminated, and Gunter slumped back in the chair to analyze the conversation.

Hotel Bar in Cleveland, Ohio

"Man, midnight in hotel bars like this is a sad time, isn't it?" Jake said to Uncle Bob.

"Okay, Boss, I'll bite, why?"

"The patrons who have paired up are for the most part happy. Those who haven't try to drink their way into a stupor."

"And your point would be?"

"It's too easy to get into a downward spiral. Which is why I'm going to call it a night."

"And leave me here to babysit the team?" Bob said with a chuckle. "You seem to have something on your mind, Boss What's bothering you?"

"Lot of the same old stuff. Wondering how long until we catch Yancy and free Joanna."

"And get the nukes back."

"Of course. I also think maybe I've been drinking a little too much lately."

"As I said before, that's understan...."

"I know what you've said, and I appreciate it. But I think it's time I got it under control and concentrated on the mission with a clear head. Think I'll go hit the sack and wake up ready to go."

"Sounds like a plan. I'll have a few more and do the same thing. See you at nine in the coffee shop."

***

Chapter 15

Jake awakened to a familiar knock on his hotel room door. *Shave and a haircut...two-bits.* No one else in Cleveland, Ohio would use that knock. It had to be Uncle Bob. He pulled the pants on he threw over a chair before going to bed. A clock on the nightstand glowed 2:39 in muted red numbers. *Must have just left the bar.*

He turned the deadbolt and pulled on the door lever. "Hey, Bob, you gonna give me another pep talk or some...."

A hammy fist from a bulky, middle-aged guy slammed into his face before he could fully deflect it. He stepped back and dropped into a fighting stance, but the fist now held a 1911 the man drew from a shoulder holster.

Jake glanced back at his service weapon sitting next to the clock.

"Don't even think about it," a voice behind the middle-aged guy warned.

"Should have answered the door with it in your hand. You should know better."

The first man shuffled aside to allow the other man to enter the room.

"Sorry about the rude introduction, Agent Thomas, but I needed to pass some information along that I didn't trust to a telephone. You of all people should know the NSA or some other alphabet agency is always listening. I'm Jack Morgan. Haven't seen you since the chopper crash in Sea Wind Bay. I'd offer to shake hands, but you might use some of that Kung Fu stuff on me."

"Jujitsu, Morgan. Hakkoryu Jujitsu."

"Right, sorry about that. By the way, why don't you call me Jack since we'll be working together. Anyway, have a seat on the bed while we talk. What should I call you?"

"I prefer Agent Thomas, and I'll stand."

The middle-aged man snapped open a collapsible baton.

"Sitting might be a better idea. Bill here may not be a black belt, but believe me, you don't want him to use that thing on you. He's an expert at putting people on crutches, or in wheelchairs."

Jake sat on the edge of the bed. "What do you want from me?"

"Nothing. In fact, I want to give you some very valuable information. You're tracking Yancy, and I can help you find him."

"Why would you, of all people, want to do that?"

"I could say I was trying to be a good citizen...."

"You? The man who faked his own death after betraying his country?"

"Yeah, I knew you wouldn't buy the good citizen thing, so let me be straight with you. I know Yancy's gone off the rails and got his hands on some nukes. He's got some ridiculous ideas about reestablishing the old Soviet Republic. That sort of thing gets in the way of my business. So, oddly enough, helping you catch him is good for me. You follow?"

"I hear you, so what's next?"

"Well, I'm aware your team is probably back in their rooms since the bar closed. You understand my dilemma, of course. I'm literally surrounded, and I need to leave without interference. So, here's my plan. Wild Bill and I get in our car and go. It's as simple as that."

"And you think I'll just let you waltz out of here?"

"That's my plan. What do you think? I know you would love to slap cuffs on me, but then you would chase Yancy all over the East Coast until a nuke or two hit a couple of major cities. You would never see your girlfriend again. Think about it, champ. I can tell you exactly where he will be in New York City."

"New York City? You think that's where he's heading?"

"Oh, for a fact. I know the street and building where he will be a few days from now. So, here's how it goes. Bill and I leave here, and one hour later I call you with the exact address. Sound good to you?"

"Do I have a choice? You seem to be running the show for the moment."

"Thankfully, yes. Now give me your phone number and wait for my call."

Morgan backed slowly toward the door while Bill checked the hallway and declared it empty.

The door closed behind them as Jake reached for his weapon. He thought about what Morgan said and sat quietly on the bed gathering his thoughts.

Uncle Bob was settling into bed ten minutes later when the phone rang.

"It's Jake. Get the team up and ready to go in ten minutes. We are heading east."

"Sure thing. Boss. How about giving them half an hour? Most of them have only had a few hours of sack time."

"Half hour will do. See you in the parking lot."

NSA Director's Satellite Phone

"This is Agent Thomas, Director."

"What can I do for you, Jake?"

"Actually, it's what I can do for you. I just got a mysterious tip from an unexpected source regarding Gregori Yancy. I had a face-to-face visit with Jack Morgan about an hour ago."

"You what? In person? Should I send a Fugitive Escort Team?"

"Not exactly. I let him go."

"You what!"

"I made a deal with him for the address in New York City where Yancy is heading."

Banner took a deep breath and let it out slowly. "I would have preferred to have him off the street, but you're the on-scene commander. I assume you played it well, and we'll leave it at that."

"Thanks, Director, I appreciate your confidence. Morgan kept his part of the deal. He just called with Yancy's address, and a little more. Says Yancy split his crew up and sent half to New York City."

"Where's the other crew going?"

"Washington, it would seem. He says he will give us the DC information in a day or two in exchange for something from us. He hinted it might have something to do with the shadowy international espionage organization we've discussed."

"The Consortium?"

"Could be, but our main focus should stay on Yancy for the moment. Suddenly it seems like Morgan might be a major player in catching him.

"Not to mention rescuing Agent Davies. It appears that like it or not, we need to work with Morgan. Is my assumption correct?"

"It's probably our best course of action. Which means I should probably split my team up. Uncle Bob can take half to New York, while I head for DC with the rest. What do you think?"

"Like I said, you're the team leader, and I'd say your instinct is right on the mark. Tell me what the personnel makeup is for each team, and what you need from me."

"Let me talk to Uncle Bob and I'll call you back."

Jake hung up and turned to Uncle Bob. "The East Coast thing is still in play, although with a twist. Find a coffee shop and we'll go over the ops."

"Your wish is my command, Boss."

Secluded Warehouse in the Bronx

"Vasily, is contact to meet us at warehouse?" Igor asked.

"Yes, but do not give address over radio."

"Is encrypted and has private line frequency. No one can hear."

"Does not matter. Yancy says do not give details over radios or sat phones, so no more talk of address."

Igor turned to his driver, "We must go faster."

Vasily interrupted, "Bad idea. You will answer to Yancy if we lose contact with rest of convoy."

"There," Vasily said ten minutes later. "Red Ford F-250, with tinted windows. Parked in lot close to entrance. Stop before truck." Vasily got out and slowly approached the vehicle.

"Was long drive from Queens," Vasily said as the driver's window on the truck slowly rolled down.

"Not as long as from Brighton."

"I am Vasily, leader of crew."

"I sorta figured that out on my own. I'm Maury. I got your wire transfer, and everything's set up, Mister Vasily."

"Vasily is first name. Sur name is of no concern to you. You keep no records of us?"

"You got it. For this kind of money, I never saw you, don't know you, and don't care what happens."

"How many empty warehouses nearby and how many full?"

"Yancy said he wanted any building within a quarter mile empty. I rent almost all the buildings around here, so I made sure. Your building is at the back of this district. The closest buildings are locked up so no one can get in."

"Is good. How many exits in building?"

"Three overhead doors on this side, all of which work. Two walk-through doors on this side of the warehouse. One is blocked. The other three sides have one door each that can be used if necessary to leave."

"You have map of local area?"

"Yeah, in case you need it for an emergency."

"Do electricity, water, and sewer work in building?"

"Yeah, yeah, yeah. All work, as well as a few added details you asked for."

Vasily smiled, took a deep breath, and slowly exhaled. "Good. Details cannot be unattended."

Maury gave his new friend an inquisitive look. "Unattended details? Ain't never heard it put that way, but whatever floats your boat."

"What does, 'floats your boat' mean?"

"What, you ain't never heard that before?" Maury watched as Vasily's expression clouded over. "It means whatever makes you happy."

Vasily relaxed. "Okay, then, it floats my boat. Let us into building. I do not wish to stand where people may see us."

Maury used a remote to open the overhead door. Vasily waived the convoy inside the warehouse after he got in the SUV.

Maury stayed outside and pressed a button on the remote to close the door and trap the Russians inside.

The convoy parked beside each other in the darkened building.

"Turn headlights on so we may see where light switches are," Vasily spoke into radio.

Headlights flared to life and illuminated a 40-man SWAT team in cover positions surrounding the parked vehicles. A voice on a bullhorn blared, "Federal agents do not move."

There was a slight pause before the staccato sound of automatic weapons erupted from the suspect vehicles and echoed off the faded brick walls of the hundred-year-old warehouse.

SWAT teams were hunkered down, and catwalks near the ceiling were lined with well-hidden snipers. Floodlights mounted on tripods burst to life and lent a movie-set quality to the scene. The acrid smell of cordite drifted in clouds in the cavernous space.

Mercenaries tried to scramble to safety, but none was to be found. This was a well-executed raid with no margin for error.

"Cease fire," Uncle Bob ordered over the bullhorn. "Vasily, you and your men are under arrest. Surrender now and nobody else gets hurt. This is your last warning." Gunfire slowly ceased. Moaning and cries of pain erupted from the suspect's vehicles.

"Give up, it's over."

Commands in Russian were relayed from one vehicle to the next.

Vasily half stepped, half fell out of the lead vehicle while firing an Uzi. "We do not surrender to American pigs," he screamed as he fell mortally wounded to the dirty concrete.

His men followed suit, and when the dust settled, the mercenaries were either dead or critically wounded.

"It's a crying shame, Agent Onkst. I hate it when they go down like that instead of giving up."

"Please, call me Bob, Captain Huser. Nobody likes a bloodbath."

"And call me Mark. I hate this outcome, no matter how bad these guys were."

The two men slowly walked around bullet-ridden vehicles. Uncle Bob opened the rear door of each box truck after carefully checking for trip wires and sensors. "I appreciate your men taking care to only fire into the cabs. My men will secure this truck if you don't mind, and please tell your men to avoid it."

"Is it that national security thing?"

"Yup," Uncle Bob offered a tight-lipped reply. He motioned for two of his team to secure the truck.

"Look, I have to leave unexpectedly Mark. I have a chopper waiting for me to join another operation in progress."

"Understood. Man, they're really running you hard. Been nice working with you."

"Likewise. Maybe next time it'll be under happier circumstances."

They shared a sarcastic laugh.

"Yeah, right." Uncle Bob grinned.

"We can always hope. I'll mop up here and forward copies of my reports, including a detailed inventory and list of the perps. And how about we have a beer next time you're in town?"

"Sounds good, and it'll be on me."

***

Chapter 16

Gunter Wilhelm's Office

"Gunter, my old friend, how are you doing?" Jack Morgan asked over the encrypted satellite phone.

"I am most assuredly not your old friend, or new friend either, for that matter. Why do you presume it is permissible to call me?" Gunter absent mindedly ran his hand over the polished, finely detailed inlay of the handcrafted desk.

"Just wanted to check in with my old buddy to see how he's getting along in his new digs. Are you settling into the god-awful heat and humidity here in Texas?"

"You said here. Does that mean you are in Houston?"

"It sure does. I came here to discuss business that shouldn't be done over the phone. How about we meet at the diner a half-mile east of the refinery main gate in an hour?"

"I have no desire to meet with you."

"I think you'll be glad you did after I explain the situation to you. Besides, if you don't, I'll send the Commissioner a packet of information that will be as good as a death warrant for you. Does that change your mind about meeting me?"

"Only marginally."

"Then how about I add that a life-changing event could happen, and, although it's not necessarily related, I'll say a name, Mike Pope."

"I'll be there." Gunter punched a button to end the call. He confirmed the door that was designed to minimize electronic surveillance was closed. He left nothing to chance with physical or communication security. Every known precaution against electronic snooping was taken, but he still felt on edge.

Maryland Interstate 95

"We go south on interstate," Yancy ordered Sasha. "Map shows twenty miles."

"*Da, Bocc.* Is good to be close. I grow weary of long drive. Is good to sleep soon."

"After warehouse is secure."

"Warehouse belongs to Consortium, *Bocc,* yet you worry is not secure?"

"What is old Russian proverb? 'Trust, but verify.' Consortium leasing man seems nervous when I talk with him, so I order investigation. So far, nothing is found, but I continue to be uneasy. Still, we have warehouse and clean new passports we will soon need. So everything is good."

"What is timeline *Bocc*?"

"Is no concern for you. I have plan."

"*Bocc*, I see *politsiya* car beside road."

"Do not worry, Sasha. They look for speeding violations...so do not speed."

Sasha stared at the State Trooper as they passed his position. The uniformed patrol officer took note and stared back.

"*Politsiya* pull out after last truck *Bocc*. I think he sees me look at him."

"What?" Yancy replied. "Too many people around to shoot you, so drive." He spoke firmly into the radio. "Do not draw attention of *politsiya*. Be careful to obey traffic laws."

The trooper closely followed the convoy for a while but did not turn on the overhead lights.

"I do not see policeman now, *Bocc*," Sasha said five minutes later. "Is he to be seen?"

"Not to me, but many trucks block my sight. Watch road and traffic." Yancy spoke into the radio. "Does anybody see *politsiya*?"

The radio squawked, "*Politsiya* car is behind me."

"Do not give him reason to stop you. Ignore him and he will soon lose interest."

The trooper pulled into the median a few minutes later and parked.

Yancy grunted and said to Sasha, "Good for you he does not follow us, so I do not shoot you."

Sasha sighed. *I must turn his attention away from me.* "We are not far from warehouse."

"*Da*, but remember, I still shoot you and give body to dogs if you make mistake again."

"I promise to be careful, *Bocc*."

Momma May's Homestyle Diner

"Gunter my old friend, how are you doing today?" Jack Morgan said with a broad smile. He put his arms up like he was going to hug Gunter Wilhelm.

Gunter backed away to avoid an embrace. "As I said on the telephone, we are not friends. What is wrong with you, anyway? We should not be meeting, much less in a public place," he replied in a near whisper as he sat down on the opposite side of a booth.

"I don't see a problem. We're just two old friends sharing a cup of coffee."

"Again, we are not friends. Furthermore, I do not have the time, nor the inclination for interaction of any kind with you." Gunter glanced around the nearly empty diner to see who might be watching.

"Don't worry. I chose this time of day because the lunch crowd is long gone. We could spot a tail a mile away."

A mousey waitress barely out of her teens interrupted, "Coffee?" She waved a half-full carafe over thick china mugs."

Gunter waved his hand to stop her in mid-sentence. "Did you not notice I was speaking?"

She took half-a-step back. "Oops, sorry."

"Geez, Gunter, she's just doing her job. You must be a real ray of sunshine in the office. We're still looking, darling, but how about some of that coffee?" Jack said.

"And for you mister?"

"Tea with sugar, and no cream." Gunter replied. He waited for her to leave. "She will undoubtedly bring a half-empty cup of tepid water and some dried-out institutional brand of tea bag. Oh, and a container of cloudy honey. You would think Americans would be more aware of the complexity of tea since this country's origins go back to the English."

"Well, yeah, Gunter, but that was a couple hundred years ago. Times do change, you know."

"Yes, I am aware of that, and please do not say my name again. How did you find this abhorrent place, anyway?" He cringed as he tried to not touch anything.

"Aw, these places have the best food anywhere. You just can't beat 'em. But back to business, and I hate to bring it up, but you owe me. After all, I saved you from yourself."

"What are you babbling about?"

Morgan reached for his shoulder holster, but stopped, as Gunter slid his hand inside his coat. "Come on, Gunter, you were burning both ends of the candle, what with working for both the CIA and the Consortium. Getting caught by one or both was a real possibility until I stepped in and saved the day. Justin, that poor little scapegoat is taking all the heat for you. The CIA and Consortium don't suspect a thing, and I bet that's the way you want to keep it, right?"

"I would be hard-pressed to argue with your statement. Since you seem to possess so much insight into Consortium operations, why has the Commissioner unexpectedly summoned me to a meeting?"

"I have a source that says they want to sweat you a little to see what pops up. Sort of a routine gut check now that you've settled into your new job. But don't worry, they can't pin anything on you."

"I cannot believe that would be the sole purpose for calling me to headquarters. You said you covered the Deer Trail event, so what else might it be?"

"Not Deer Trail. I made sure it can't be traced back to either of us."

"Either of us? It was all you and Yancy."

"Okay, then if you prefer, none of us. We smell like roses my friend. Yancy, not so much, but we'll let him deal with that."

The waitress brought their drinks but stayed away from Gunter as much as possible. "Anything else?"

"Thanks, I think that's all for now," Jack replied over the sound of clattering silverware and dishes as a busboy cleared tables around them. Morgan watched him for a moment to see if he was eavesdropping, then relaxed when he moved on.

Gunter wiped the spoon with a napkin before stirring sugar into his tea.

Morgan cleared his throat and became serious. "You see, my friend, I know what you want."

"And what is that?"

"Power, and not just the supervisory role you have now. You want Commissioner level power, and I can get if for you. As Assistant Commissioner, you would answer only to me. I know what motivates you and I can give it to you."

"Do you really believe that to be so? Do you forget the Consortium already has leaders? You may be able to accomplish some things, but taking over the Consortium would be far-fetched, even for you. What would convince me to support you?"

"Well, for a start, the thirty-eight million, four hundred twenty-six thousand three hundred twelve dollars and forty-nine cents, as of yesterday, that you've stolen from the Consortium over the years."

Gunter shoved himself back in the booth as a pale shocked look slowly spread across his face. It was quickly replaced with one of defiance. "You have no proof...."

"Oh, but I do. Lost your poker face for a moment there, didn't you? Look, I don't blame you for stealing the money. I blame the Consortium for not protecting it from you. That will never happen when you work for me because I won't put you in a position to be able to. Besides, I pay so much better than they do, you won't need to. And with me, you lie, you die."

"I have no need to lie. What I did is the

nature of the business. So, the only unexpected thing is that you have information regarding those accounts. I make no apologies. Do you intend to betray me to the Consortium?"

Morgan laughed. "No, quite the contrary. Although I did want to see how you would react to the threat. Like I said, I couldn't care less about the money. However, I would have shot you here and now if you lied to me. Nothing is more important to me than trust. Don't ever forget that. Your life depends on it."

"What will you do with my overseas accounts?"

"Nothing, since I don't care about Consortium money. Consider it a signing bonus from me."

"You assume I will join you. Have you forgotten about the CIA?"

"How could I forget about those clowns? Actually, I want you to keep that iron in the fire since it might prove helpful to us in the future."

Jack picked up his cup, blew on it and leaned back in the booth. He sat upright a minute later. "Well, buddy, I hate to run, but I am very busy. I'll give you a day or two to consider my offer. Don't wait too long, though. I need to know what to do with your dossier." He stood, tossed a twenty-dollar bill on the table, and left.

Gunter sat in deep thought for a few minutes. He switched the twenty for a five and walked out.

Warehouse District, Georgetown, MD

"Is ahead on left, Sasha. Go slow, I want to see contact before we drive in lot."

"What vehicle do we look for, *Bocc*?"

"Yellow Mustang convertible. I do not like this. Is too flashy. Consortium representative should blend in."

"Two cars together in lot, *Bocc*."

"Should be one only. This I also do not like. Stop here, Sasha so I may call contact before we enter."

Yancy dialed as the small convoy of cargo trucks and SUV's stopped behind him. "Weldon, is this you in Mustang?" He put his hand over the mouthpiece of the phone and said to Sasha, "What is this name Weldon?"

Sasha shrugged.

Yancy's continued, "Why do you bring men? I say only you, so send them away." He stared out the windshield of the SUV with his face twisted in anger.

A tall thin man in a three-piece suit exited the passenger side of the Mustang and walked slowly and deliberately toward Yancy's vehicle. His jacket flapped open to reveal an automatic pistol stuffed in his waistband. He stopped just short of the SUV.

Yancy left the passenger door open as he slowly exited the SUV. He leaned back in to whisper, "Be ready."

He stood and addressed the man in the three-piece suit, "Why do you have gun?"

"It is necessary in our business."

"Perhaps. What is codeword?"

"Absolve."

"*Da*, reply is doubtless," Yancy said with a steely stare that was returned.

"You told me you were thirty minutes out when you called."

"Traffic on 495 is like fish hatchery in old country. All fish…no water."

"Never heard that one before. I would have given you better directions had I known far enough ahead of time." He extended a bony arm and shook hands.

"Warehouse is ready?"

"It is. We can go inside and get you settled in anytime you want."

The men returned to their cars as an overhead garage door opened to allow the convoy to enter.

***

Chapter 17

Georgetown Warehouse

A key in the lock of the secure storeroom woke Joanna in an instant. Her eyes popped open but saw nothing in the almost total darkness of the windowless space. "Who's there?" she mumbled.

A flip of a light switch outside the door flooded the room with blinding florescent light. Joanna put an arm over her eyes. "Could you turn some of that light off, please, or at least give me sunglasses? I've been in the dark since I got here." Her eyes adjusted to the light enough to reveal the silhouette of a man in the doorway. "How much longer are you going to keep me here?"

"You will be released soon if your boyfriend cooperates."

"Boyfriend?"

"Agent Thomas. Do not play coy with me. He is the only reason you still breathe."

"And who are you?"

"I am Gregori Yancy. I used you to lure Thomas here."

"Okay, but why?"

"We have history for which I must kill him."

"Jake? What kind of history?"

"He kills my brother."

"I don't know anything about that."

"Was long time ago, but I never forget. Old Russian proverb says keep friends close, but enemies closer. He will search for you."

"I thought that was an old Mafia saying."

"They steal from Russians. I must know where Thomas and BlackStar Ops Group team is so I may avoid them while I carry out my mission."

"Okay, maybe it's the lack of sleep, or the drugs you've been pushing into me, but I don't understand. You make it sound like a military operation."

"Is correct. I am here to destroy your seat of government."

"Wait, are you saying we're in Washington? Why?"

"Again, do not be coy. You know I have nukes. I intend to strike at the very heart of US."

"Haven't you heard, the Cold War is over."

"For some maybe, but not for true Russian patriot."

"Yes, but the old system is going away."

"But is not gone. Attack on US by agent of Mother Russia could bring other countries back so Union of Soviet Socialist Republics will live again." Yancy's voice rose to a near shout.

Joanna involuntarily shrunk away. "Do you hear your own voice? I know you can kill me if you want, but somebody has to tell you the truth. What you're going for is an impossible dream. Give it up and I'm sure our government will work with you."

"You must listen to your voice. I do not surrender, for my name will live for eternity."

"What do you want from me?"

"Talk to boyfriend. Make him know I will kill you if he does not stop."

"I doubt that will have much effect on him. Like you, he is mission oriented. He will not stop until you are captured or dead."

"Call me romantic, but I am sure he will not let you die. Now I must return to office."

"Look, Yancy, I don't like this any more than you," Jack Morgan's distorted voice came through the encrypted phone in

Yancy's office. "But now that I've laid out what's going on, can you see why it's advantageous for us to work together?"

"If what you say is true about Consortium, is good to have ally."

"So, now that I know about your mission, what can I do for my new friend?"

"Maybe nothing…maybe something. I may need extraction if infernal BlackStar Ops Group discovers my location. I do not trust some of my men. You and I answer to Consortium. This makes me confident you will honor deal."

"I certainly understand. Tell you what, I'll have my man Johnson waiting in a van for the next five days. All Consortium properties have built-in escape routes…."

"*Da,* Weldon shows me."

"Good. Wild Bill will wait in a white van in the parking lot next door. Simply call when you are ready for a pickup. I suppose you want the usual exit strategy?"

"I must disappear without trace."

"We can do that."

NSA Headquarters, Fort Meade, MD

"Welcome to DC," John Banner started the call with Jake Thomas.

"Thanks, Director, although we're still twenty miles out. Any word on Yancy and crew?"

"Not specifically. Morgan says he will give us the location tomorrow at noon."

"Why noon?"

"No idea, and he wouldn't say. Guy is a real crackpot, but I hope he keeps his word anyway."

"You and me both. We'll settle into an agency hotel and get some sleep."

"Good luck with that, but at least rest. I imagine the next few days are going to be a little stressful."

"We can take the stress if the mission succeeds. He have anything on Joanna?"

"Not definitive. We can only pray she's okay. I'll talk to you first thing in the morning unless something comes up. In the meantime, goodnight, Jake and stay strong."

"I will for her. Goodnight, Director."

Jake ended the call and mumbled, "She's okay, or Yancy is a dead man."

"Sorry, Boss, did you say something?" the agent driving asked.

"No, just thinking out loud. Let's get to the hotel and settle in."

Georgetown, Maryland

"I need keys to van," Sasha said in a timid voice.

"What, you do not call me *Bocc?* I think you forget your place."

"Sorry, *Bocc.* I have uncle in hospital I worry about, so mind wanders. I will not forget again who I work for."

"That would serve you well. Why is it you need keys?"

"I must move van to make room for trucks."

"Do not worry, for there is enough room for trucks. Is not your concern."

"I try to take more responsibility in absence of Vasily."

Yancy eyed him for a moment with one eyebrow raised. "I make you temporary supervisor because Vasily is not here. Do you wish to replace him?"

Sasha stared at the floor before mumbling, "No...yes...maybe. I can be good supervisor."

Yancy leaned his head back and guffawed. "Now truth comes out. Ambition is good, but I do not replace Vasily soon. Perhaps someday. Until then, you must follow orders."

"*Da, Bocc*. When do we leave?"

"I tell you when I wish for you to know. Again, is no concern for you. Leave me now." Yancy stared at Sasha as he walked out and left the door slightly ajar.

One Block from the Warehouse

"Mother," Sasha spoke quietly into the payphone.

"Yes, my son. Are you well?"

"I am good, Mother. How is Uncle Maxim?"

"He is so sick. You will come soon?"

"This I do not know. I am told we finish job in few days and leave, but do not stay close. Men in crew say there is hidden reason to leave."

Sasha nonchalantly shuffled around and shifted from side to side to see if he was being watched.

"Is too bad. I want to see my son."

"Is unfortunate other men travel to New York, but not me. But *Bocc* pays well, so I do not complain. Vasily is away in New

York City, so *Bocc* gives me temporary supervisor position. Is getting late. I must return to warehouse now."

"You will call soon?"

"When work allows."

"Be careful. Family sends love."

Sasha hung up the phone and searched for surveillance. Dogs barked behind security fences. Traffic hummed on an elevated highway nearby, and sirens went about their urgent business as Sasha slowly strode back to the warehouse.

Georgetown Warehouse

"Sasha, come to office," Yancy spoke into the two-way radio. "Bring Alexi with you."

"Yes, *Bocc*?" Sasha hurried in with Alexi.

"I have special job."

"What is it you need to be done?"

"You and Alexi must wear these." He pointed to folded uniforms on a table. "Magnetic signs for white panel van are under them. Signs and uniforms belong to company which services elevators. You will mount metal box from crate in van to top of elevator in Washington Monument."

"Forgive that I ask, *Bocc,* but what is in box?"

Yancy stood and pounded his fists on the old metal desk. His voice rose an octave higher, "Is no concern for you. Do not open box if you wish to avoid painful death."

"*Da, Bocc*, we follow orders."

"Put these stickers on box after you mount on elevator." Yancy scowled and tossed some large white stickers that read *High Voltage, Danger, Do Not Open under Penalty of Law,* and *Authorized Personnel Only*.

He continued, "Give paperwork to guard. Consortium experts forge work order so it will not be questioned. If guard calls number for company, they will verify work order. Take MiG welder to seal bolts when box is mounted."

"We will not fail you."

"Is good for you. Failure means pain and certain death." Yancy leaned back in the chair and gave the men an icy stare.

"We know job is important, *Bocc*."

"Is good you know, Sasha. Monument closes to public at 5 PM. Director is at fundraising party then. I have operative who insures he does not answer pager. She is very persuasive."

Washington Monument

Sasha pulled the white panel van up to a heavy metal chain draped across pylons at the entrance to the delivery area. A uniformed guard holding a clipboard left the guard shack and ambled toward them.

"Sorry, gentlemen, unless this is a service call, you'll have to come back tomorrow."

"Is urgent service order for work to be done on elevator."

"Can't let you in unless I got you on the schedule, fellas, and I don't see no elevator work here." He pointed to the clipboard. "It's against the rules unless it's an emergency."

"But you must have work order. Please be so kind to check again."

The guard sighed and slowly returned to the shack. He rifled through paperwork on another clipboard and shuffled back to the van. "There is an order here, but it says you were supposed to be here at 4 PM. Watchful Eye Electronics is usually very prompt. What are you supposed to do anyway?"

"We install new electronic security system onto elevator. Is very delicate, so we must limit travel. Orders from boss are to install today."

The armed guard stared at them for a moment, huffed, and mumbled under his breath. He fumbled with a key ring on his belt and found the right one. The heavy black chain fell to the asphalt with a clanking sound.

Sasha drove slowly toward the monument while the guard reset the barricade. He stopped the van after a few car lengths and rolled the window down. "Crate is heavy. You and other guard can help, yes?"

"You're kidding, right?"

"System is delicate. Fall would damage it. Should be another man, but he calls in sick."

The guard stared at his partner. What do you think, should we give them a hand?"

"Sure, why not?" the younger guard replied. "Had an argument with my girlfriend this morning and missed my workout. Should be getting paid extra for this, but what the heck, doesn't look all that heavy," he said as he hefted a corner. "Naw, put one of us on each corner and it's a piece of cake."

Sasha looked at Alexi, shrugged his shoulders and turned back to the guards. "I will make note in report of generous help."

The four men gently carried the crate into the monument after one of the guards unlocked the service door.

Alexi leaned close to Sasha's ear. "You are genius to get guards help."

"Is old tool I use. Be polite and say you need help. People in this country wish to be liked, so they help."

"Is good. Does *Bocc* say what is box?"

"*Nyet*. But must be important. He says do not drop or molest."

"Should one of us stay to keep an eye on them?" the younger guard quietly asked.

"Why? Elevator's locked down, and ain't nothing in the lobby they can steal."

The guards returned to their post, and Sasha and Alexi spent most of the next hour mounting the box on top of the elevator.

"Box will not hit anything as it goes up and down," Alexi noted.

"It will also not be easy to access during routine maintenance," Sasha replied. "So welded attachment points will not be seen. We must now place fake warning stickers on box."

"Is good job."

"Now, for fun, we have guard sign work order." Sasha smiled as they walked toward the guard shack. "Wait for best part."

The younger guard noted the time on the log out sheet and signed it. "There you go, champ. Now sign next to me."

"Yes, and many thanks for help."

"What the heck kind of name is that? Sounds Russky to me. Where were you born?"

"St. Petersburg. Mother is American, father is Russian."

"Okay, but what is your first name?"

"George, to honor father."

"Whatever. Have a nice day."

"I did not know you have sense of humor," Alexi said as they drove away. "But what would you do if he says name out loud?"

"Most Amerikansky do not try to say foreign names."

"Is good, but how do you think of *Dzhordz Vashington*?"

"I think George Washington in Russian is good joke."

***

Chapter 18

Washington Monument, Washington, DC

"Ok, kids, let's everybody stay together," Nancy Groff told her third-grade class from Elkhart, Indiana, as she herded them down from the third-floor landing.

"I'll lead the children if you'll bring up the rear, so we don't lose any of them," the tour guide offered. *Karen*, with no last name, had been punched out with a label maker and taped over another name on the tag she wore.

"Sounds great, I appreciate you doing this for us. It took a lot of wrangling to get the private tour down from the third floor to see all the plaques on the wall. I'll try and keep them quiet while you explain everything."

Karen grinned. "We'll see what we can do about the quiet part. I love giving this tour to the kids. It's something they'll remember for the rest of their lives."

The two shepherded their young charges down the black metal stairwell as Karen explained the plaques mounted on the wall. "These plaques were donated by state and civic organizations while the monument was being built. Of course, I'm sure they were accompanied by large sums of money."

Her attempt at subtle humor brought no reaction from the children, so she continued, "Okay then, here we are on the second-floor landing. This stone was donated by the Franklin Fire Company of Washington D.C., and this one from the National Grey's. That one was given by the Washington National Monument Society. All three were donated in 1850."

"Who donated the metal box on top of the elevator?" a tall, lanky redheaded boy asked as he pressed himself into the chain-link fence around the elevator shaft.

"What metal box?" Karen's voice took on a stern tone, "You should be looking at the wall like the rest of the class."

The tour group turned and crowded around the elevator shaft. "It has blinking red lights," the redheaded boy added.

"Something's blinking?" Karen asked, more out of curiosity than anything. "Wow, that's a new one on me. Why would it be blinking?" She pulled a two-way radio from her belt, twisted a dial, and spoke into the mike in a voice that was supposed to sound, calm and nonchalant. "Uh, this is Karen Nelson on the second-floor landing. Is there supposed to be a large metal box with a blinking red light on top of the elevator?"

The maintenance supervisor replied with a note of skepticism, "Don't know what you're talking about, lady. Ain't supposed to be no box on top of the elevator car. It would block the emergency exit on top.

279

Even if there was one, it wouldn't have no blinking red lights."

"Then could you tell me what I'm looking at?" Karen said in a voice that was now a little defensive. "Look, I know I'm new here, but I've never seen it before. And the blinking red light just changed to red numbers counting down. What should I do?"

The supervisor's skepticism turned to concern. "What does it look like?" She described the box in detail. "Let me check a few things out and I'll call you back."

I-95

"I don't understand how Morgan stays one

step ahead of us," Jake said to Uncle Bob in the darkened interior of the SUV. He yawned and stretched as much as possible.

"You read his file. Twenty years in the DEA gave him a lot of contacts and skills."

"I know. He planned and directed operations all over the country. What happened to make him turn to the other side? Was it money, or revenge?"

"Maybe he was passed over for promotion too many times. Plus, the appeal of easy money in the drug trade could do it."

"It's possible, but I think it goes deeper than that. After all, power can be a strong aphrodisiac."

"True, but what worries me is I don't see him being loyal to any particular country or ideology. So, what's his end game?"

"Hard to say. He dropped all the way off the radar after Sea Wind Bay. Although Bart said he thought he saw Morgan after the attack on Cheyenne Mountain. John Banner's been warning us he might pop up, and now it looks like he has."

"I guess we have to play his game for now. Right, Boss?"

"At least until we have enough intel to figure out what he's up to," Jake said as he stared out the window.

GoldStar Refinery, Houston Texas

Gunter pulled a two-way radio from the charging station in an antique armoire in his office. "Mister Ballard, would you come to my office, please?"

"On my way."

"You want to see me," Jim said as he entered the office.

"I have been advised of a Board of Directors meeting next week in Switzerland which requires my attendance."

"I didn't realize you were a member of the Board of Directors."

"Indeed I am. Among other topics, I shall be addressing the status of the refinery, and timeline for its reconstitution."

"I'm guessing you'll be needing an updated timeline from me for the meeting?"

"I will. I also have an extremely important shipment coming in next week I thought I would be handling personally. It is a guarded shipment of proprietary equipment that cannot be left unattended in a warehouse. Therefore, I need for you to receive and secure it."

"Sounds easy enough."

"On the contrary, it must be safeguarded with your very life."

"My life? Makes it sound like it's worth billions."

"I suppose it does, and that is not far from the truth. It is vital to our operations. There will be two truckloads of wooden crates that must not be opened by anyone but me. I will allow access to a secure storage areas in my building to complete the task."

"Thought I already had access…."

"As facility manager you have access to the building. However, there are a few areas that are restricted. You understand proprietary operations, so I assume you understand."

"Yeah, I guess so. Just caught me by surprise. Not a problem. Those crates will be safer than a bug in a rug. They won't leave my sight from the time they arrive until they're locked in the secure storage room."

"Thank you, Jim. I knew I could count on you. Use only highly trusted men to move the shipment, and only enough to get the job done. Keep the crates together at all times."

"Sounds like a top-secret mission for the government, or something."

"Think of it as such and you shall not go wrong. Furthermore, I do not want Jaeger involved in any aspect of the operation. In fact, I want him to remain as unaware of the shipment as possible. Now back to business.

I need the updated timetable Monday. I do not yet know the exact day I travel, but it is usually mid-week."

Jim rubbed his chin and stared at the ceiling for a moment. "I'll need two days to put it down on paper since I know how you like detail. Appraising the whole operation from top to bottom will more'n likely take up the day before that. Shouldn't be a problem."

"Very good. I have come to appreciate your thorough approach to my requests."

"Least I can do with what you pay me," Jim said over his shoulder as he left."

NSA Director's Office

"I have to admit this is a little surreal," John Banner said to Jake Thomas.

"How so, Director?" Jake replied as he reached for a mug of coffee on the side table next to a comfortable armchair.

"I'm accustomed to being parked here in my office while subordinates run ops all over the world. But now the action is right in my backyard. Actually, more like my front yard. What do you need to stop the threat?"

"Intel on Yancy's location and a SWAT team. You going to take over the op?"

"Absolutely not. You are doing such an outstanding job I want you to continue. Let me answer this call and we'll devise a plan."

"Sure."

"Well, that's good news. Our signals intel people tracked down a pattern of phone and radio calls connected to the intel Onkst picked up from the leasing agent in New York. We have pinned the location down to a two-block radius in Georgetown. The team I put on alert is ready to go with ten minutes notice. You ready to go get Joanna back?"

"More than you'll ever know."

Washington Monument

A hollow voice on the radio announced, "This is Security. Thought you'd like to know, we're coming to check out the box on the elevator."

Karen did not try to hide the fear in her voice, "Please hurry...the timer says eighty-nine minutes and forty-three seconds."

"Get your group out of there now."

Karen forced a smile. "Listen up, kids," she said in a shaky voice, "We're going down the stairs and outside like a fire drill in school. Stay together, and don't dawdle. Missus Groff, would you please take up the rear?"

The young tour guide led the frightened group through the lobby as three security guards ran past them up the stairs.

"Follow Missus Groff onto the bus," Karen ordered. "Wake up the driver and tell him to get as far away from here as he possibly can. Don't stop for anything," she said to the teacher in a voice that was barely above a whisper. "I don't know what's in that box, but my daddy would probably say nothing good."

"What does your daddy do?"

"Police lieutenant back home."

The concerned teacher used thirty years of experience to direct the children. "We need to get on the bus right now." The children complied, and she turned back to Karen, "Aren't you coming with us?"

"No. You don't need my help, and I need to stay here to help."

Missus Groff nodded and offered a wan smile as she mounted the steps.

Karen smiled back and waved as the driver closed the accordion style doors.

***

Chapter 19

NSA Director's Office

"Come in," Banner replied to a knock on the door.

A tall figure dressed in black tactical gear entered the room. "We're on standby, sir. Any idea how soon you'll need us? Hey, Jake, you doin' okay?"

"As well as can be expected, Eric. We're facing hardened mercenaries led by a highly trained spy on a mission. Don't expect them to just lay down their weapons. Pretty sure it will get rough, so having an SRT with us is probably a good idea."

"We can handle it, especially if you're running point. Let me know when it's a go."

"Now is as good as anytime. We have reliable intel on Yancy's location, so let's go take him down."

Eric turned to the Director. "What are the SYSOP limits? Is it capture or kill?"

"Too many national secrets are involved for a public trial. Yancy's got to be silenced. Do you have a problem with that?"

"Have I ever?" Eric replied. "I'll do whatever it takes to recover our agent and the nukes."

"You know how I feel after he took Joanna," Jake added. "Thing is, I don't understand why he would drag her halfway across the country, instead of just killing her outright. This feels personal, like he wants to torture me." He choked and coughed to cover it as tears glistened in his eyes.

Banner spoke after an awkward moment, "We are still trying to put the Yancy puzzle together with a lot of missing pieces. It appears he is targeting you for reasons that aren't clear at this point. Any thoughts?"

"None. As far as I know, we have never even met. I mean, breaking up the Sea Wind Bay operation probably cost him a small fortune. I'm sure that caused him a lot of heartburn. But I don't see how that would put me at the top of his list."

"Unless there is a deeper motivation."

"Doesn't matter one way or another. I can't let it get in the way of capturing him. If he's the deep-cover Cold War spy we think he is, he won't go down easy."

Banner sighed. "After all he's done, from the Mather op until now, you are probably right."

"Mather," Eric said with a puzzled look. "I thought Rick Eichner did that, not Yancy. I'm a little confused."

Banner sat back in his chair and looked back and forth from Jake to Eric before replying, "It doesn't leave this room, but we think there are other forces at play here. Eichner was only the tip of the iceberg. Intel suggests there is another, much larger organization behind it."

"But the Soviets are out of the picture, aren't they?"

"Yes, but we suspect remnants of the old Soviet Union intel service are involved directly or indirectly."

"Russia says they dissolved their connections to the Soviet Bloc intel community," Jake replied. "Surely, they wouldn't lie to us, now, would they?"

"Right. But sarcasm aside, you hit on a key point. They were our sworn adversaries for half-a-century. Regardless of Gorbachov and his make-nice posturing, most of the internal structure of the Soviet intel community is still alive and well. They may have changed the name of their agencies, but it's still the same old team at work."

"And working closely with their old allies in a dozen countries," Jake replied. "Have we been able to identify who this other organization is?"

"Matter of fact, we have strong indications that a powerful combination of old allies is working out of Switzerland. They provide services to private and government agencies around the globe."

Jake smiled. "Switzerland, huh? Clever to locate in a country that claims to be neutral."

"Switzerland doesn't fall all over themselves claiming to be our friends, or of anybody else, for that matter. We also know this spy organization has regional headquarters around the world."

Eric broke in, "Even in the US?"

"More or less. We think they based their North American operation in Toronto until recently. It suddenly closed down, and we are trying to determine where it is now."

"Could be anywhere," Jake noted. "It doesn't take a lot of space to run operations."

"They could disguise their computer work as a telemarketing call center or financial services company," the Director replied. "We just don't have enough info to go on at this point in time."

"Which leaves the question open as to whether Yancy is running this op for himself, or...."

Jake was interrupted by Tim, his communications tech bursting into the room.

"Boss, a 911 call just came in from the Washington Monument describing a suspicious device that sounds an awful lot like a BlackStar system."

"Thanks, Tim. Any details?"

"No. What we have so far is from intercepts on emergency services comm links."

"Okay. Director, we're in your office, so it's your call. How do you want to handle it?"

"I told you before, Jake, you are in charge of the team. You decide."

"All right then, Bob Onkst is on the way here from New York by chopper. Tim, have the Situation Room divert him to the monument to assess the situation. Eric, we need to raid the Georgetown location now."

"No problem," Eric responded. "I pre-positioned Rapid Response Teams at three points in the city, fully staffed and ready to roll. Closest one is at the other end of the National Mall from the monument. Another is five minutes away from Yancy's location. They can be there in five minutes or less. I also have a chopper on the pad that will get us there at about the same time."

"Sounds like you have it under control. Good job."

"Simply following your plan. Now, if you're ready, we need to move out."

"Director, we'll stay in touch over comms. Want to come with us and play?"

"Love to, but somebody needs to mind the store. Good luck, gentlemen, and let's all go home at the end of the day."

"That's always our goal, Director."

Georgetown Warehouse

The SRT team stayed out of sight a block from Yancy's suspected location. Their response vehicle was disguised as a five-ton utility company work truck. A team member wearing a yellow hard hat adjusted the toolbelt around his waist and scrambled up a utility pole. "S-7 in place," he said into his comm mike.

"Affirmative, S-7," a communications tech inside the truck replied. "SITREP?"

"Two figures at each end of the front of the structure trying very hard to look as nonchalant as possible."

"How's that working for them?"

"Terrible, I spotted them in a heartbeat. No visual inside the building. Looks like the windows have been painted over."

"Any other perps visible?"

"Can't see the back and opposite end of the structure, but nobody at this end."

"Confirm, S-7. Maintain position and try to look busy."

The communications tech said to Jake Thomas, "No other subjects located by one of our guys posing as a jogger."

"Has the local PD cordoned off the area for three blocks?"

"Yes, sir."

"Good. Then I'd say it's time to knock on the door and introduce ourselves. Sergeant Wilson, is your team ready?"

"Ready as a socialite on Saturday night."

"Not sure what that means, but let's hit the bricks. First, though, have the snipers hit the two lookouts in front of the building."

Wilson issued quiet commands into his comm unit. Both mercenaries simultaneously fell mortally wounded thirty seconds later.

Jake pushed the double doors at the back of the rig open and jumped to the gritty pavement. His rubber-soled utility boots made almost no noise. He was followed by ten NSA SRT team members.

Another ten members came out of a fake bread delivery truck at the other end of the building. A big brown delivery truck around the corner disgorged ten more. They formed single lines that silently converged on one side and the front of the building.

A hefty team member with a battering ram stood ready at the single-person entry door.

Jake nodded and watched as the door exploded inward. The man dropped the ram and shouldered his weapon.

Jake stepped into the dark interior and shuffled to the left to clear the doorway for those who followed. The next man in the stack advanced no more than two paces before shots rang out.

Jake heard the dull metallic splat of rounds hitting the man's ballistic armor. He sprayed the building with an M-4 rifle equipped with night vision capability.

The battering ram team member stepped through the door, took a round to the leg and went down.

Jake pulled him behind a vehicle as other SRT team members poured into the building. One moved along the wall and hit a button to open an overhead door.

A ten-man team rushed through and took up defensive positions. Gunfire echoed throughout the building.

Light from the open overhead door showed Yancy and two of his men herding Joanna between them as they descended from an office on the upper level.

Jake moved toward the stairs in a crouching position.

Yancy stopped at the base of the steps and pulled Joanna to him with one arm around her neck. He held a pistol to her head and shouted, "Stay back, or I splatter walls with her brains."

Jake kept his weapon against his shoulder with Yancy's forehead in the sights as he shuffled forward.

"Do you think I kid you?" Yancy said in a gravelly voice. "Stop, or she dies."

Jake paused for a split-second as Yancy and his men dragged Joanna toward a small door further down the wall. A scene from the recurring nightmare flashed through his mind. *This can't be happening!* He shook off the thought and advanced toward the mercenaries.

One of Yancy's men raised his weapon, but it never made it above waist level when two shots in quick succession struck his chest and forehead. He was dead before he landed face first on the grimy concrete floor.

The other mercenary met the same fate when he tried to fire at Jake.

"It's your choice, *Comrade.* Surrender now or go out of here feet first."

"If I do, she goes first," Yancy defiantly answered as he ducked and weaved behind her.

Jake could not come up with a firing solution with Joanna shielding Yancy.

Frustration built inside him, but he stayed calm.

Suddenly, in one swift move, Joanna raised her right foot and raked down Yancy's shin with her heel. She finished the move by stomping on his instep.

Yancy yowled in pain and almost fell. Instead, he released her, and pushed his way through the steel door.

Joanna tried to drop down to give Jake a clear shot and accidently tripped Yancy.

Jake instinctively aimed lower just as Yancy recovered from a stumble and stood. The round struck Yancy's leg instead of his chest before the door closed. The metallic sound of a lock closing echoed through the warehouse.

Jake scooped Joanna up in his arms and brushed hair back from her face. "Nice move."

"Thanks. I'm okay," she said through clenched teeth. Now go get the bastard."

"I'm a medic, and I have her," a voice behind Jake declared.

"Go," Joanna shouted. "Don't let him get away."

The door yielded on the third kick, but only opened part way. Jake squeezed through with a half-dozen team members behind him.

Inside the Washington Monument

"Why are we standing here watching a timer count down instead of hauling ass out of here?" a security guard asked his partner. "That thing is probably a bomb, so why are we sticking around?"

"Because it's our job, dipstick. Although I have to admit, I wish I was up in my cabin at the lake instead of standing here with your sorry butt. So, what do we do now?"

"Manual says call 911 and evacuate." He keyed the mike on his radio. "Front Desk, hit the fire alarm to evacuate the building. Then call 911 and tell them we have a suspicious device on top of the elevator."

"You sure?" a tinny voice came back.

"Never been more sure in my life, darling, so do it now, hear? Timer just passed through eighty-eight minutes."

"Yes, sir, but you need to tell me right now if this is a drill or not. Otherwise, you take the blame if it turns out to be false."

"Believe me, this is no drill, and I take full responsibility."

A few seconds later an ear-splitting klaxon sounded, and strobe lights flashed. The security guards stared at the timer as it counted down through eighty-seven minutes, one second at a time.

"Unit 1, this is Dispatch…you still in the monument?"

"Sure am. Where's that bomb unit?"

"Well, that's the thing, it's sort of on hold…."

"What the…? We're sitting on top of what could be a bomb in the middle of one of the most sacred places in the country, and we're on hold? What in the world is going on?"

"Don't know. Got a call from higher-ups saying a specialized team will be there in less than ten minutes."

"Whatever, but I'm getting real nervous here. Ten minutes is gonna feel like a lifetime."

***

Chapter 20

Georgetown Warehouse

Yancy bolted through the steel exit door into the cavernous warehouse next door. It was filled with industrial shelves holding a variety of rusty parts covered with dust. He struggled to knock over a free-standing metal shelving unit at least ten-foot tall and finally heaved it onto its side. The contents scattered onto the damp floor and partially blocked the door. *That must slow them down.*

He headed to the other side of the warehouse, but the gunshot wound gave him a staggered lope that made it difficult to run. An old furnace vent on the wall had a lever made to look like a simple armature in disrepair. The leasing agent had shown him it was actually a lock that opened the vent cover and led to an exit.

Yancy used his body weight to hoist the cover to expose a four-foot-tall tunnel that slanted down to a storm sewer. He carefully closed the vent behind him and stumbled half-stooped over the length of the concrete pipe. A slight bend in the passageway revealed daylight at the end that grew brighter with every step. Closer inspection showed that it discharged into the Potomac River.

The wounded spy nearly lost his balance as he leaned out of the sewer pipe on his knees and carefully surveyed the area for witnesses. The pipe extended well over the riverbank and dumped a nauseating trickle into the scummy water below.

He tried to sit down, slipped, and fell face first into the fetid water in the pipe. He managed to roll onto his side and gently extend his legs out, hoping to hang onto the rim before dropping the five feet or so to the riverbank.

The injured mercenary braced his good arm on one side and tried to carefully lower himself. But the rim was coated with slimy sludge that caused him to lose his grip.

Yancy fell to the edge of the riverbank and rolled into the icy water. The rocks lining the river were slick with a coating of moss that hindered his every move.

He struggled for purchase and managed to belly-crawl his way up the embankment. It was steep, but he made it after considerable time and effort. *I will stand out like sore thumb with muck and moss that covers me.*

The van that should be in the parking lot next door held his own personal escape kit. He desperately needed a change of clothes, some medical supplies, a bag of cash, and the stash of weapons that were in it. Most importantly, a driver would be waiting. Yancy's wounds would severely limit his ability to drive.

The postal facility ran 24-hours a day, 7-days a week, so a windowless cargo van in the parking lot would not draw attention.

Yancy's stealth training in the former Soviet Union paid off. He covered his tracks, stayed out of the mud, and made a mental note not to snap twigs off trees as he stumbled through them.

If he had not been injured, he might have considered making his way upriver. But that would require him to move slowly as his loss of blood steadily increased. It made getting to the van key to his survival.

Damnable BlackStar Ops team.. A search would quickly expose the escape tunnel and narrow their search parameters. It would not take long to cordon off the area.

Yancy made it to the edge of the parking lot and immediately spotted the plain white van parked a hundred feet away by some semi-trailers. He glanced at his Rolex and frantically patted his pockets looking for his cell phone. *Where could it be?*

Dozens of people mingled in the parking lot. He would be spotted if he stumbled through the open area but could not wait and lose more blood.

The woods supplied enough cover to avoid detection, and Yancy moved as fast as he could with an injured leg. A distant sound of barking dogs could be a search team, or maybe just local dogs. He could not wait to find out.

Time was not on his side. Time since the shootout. More time moving through the storm sewer. Even more time lost stumbling through the woods. Yancy was getting desperate and would have to make his own luck.

He stood up straight and shuffled toward the parked van. Several people stared, and one asked, "You okay, dude?"

Yancy ignored them as he headed straight to the getaway vehicle. He grabbed the handle of the passenger side door, but it would not budge.

He started to pound on the window but stopped with his fist frozen in mid-air. The driver was slumped open-mouthed in the seat with eyes wide open in a death stare.

What now? His head swiveled frantically from side to side. A handful of bystanders ambled toward him. *Should I steal a vehicle? Maybe I should say I was in accident and must go to hospital.*

The side door ground open with a grinding clatter, and a strong arm pulled him onto the floor of the van next to another lifeless body.

A masked figure slammed the door shut and pulled the body out of the driver's seat to take his place. The engine started, and the van backed quickly toward the curious bystanders. They scattered, and the driver executed a respectable one hundred and eighty degree turn to head toward the river.

"*Nyet,*" Yancy yelled. "We must leave this place."

The driver turned his head and stated clearly through the mask, "Stay calm, Mister Yancy. This is part of the plan."

Yancy grabbed the back of the seat for balance as the van bumped and rocked over the back curb and out of the parking lot.

His rescuer skillfully guided the vehicle around trees back in the direction of the warehouse. Yancy started to object but realized it must also be part of the plan.

The van came to an abrupt halt pointing downhill toward the river. The masked man put the dead man back behind the wheel and placed the other body in the passenger seat. He opened the side door and ushered Yancy out.

His rescuer ran to the driver's door, slipped the van into drive, and stepped aside. The van gathered speed until it hit the dark swirling water with an explosive splash. It floated for a short while before disappearing nose down into the current.

Washington Monument

The timer continued its relentless downward trek. Security guards stared at the device as if by sheer concentration they could make it stop.

They both jumped as the two-way radio squawked to life. "Unit 1, this is Dispatch. PD is setting up barricades up and down the mall, and FD has crews on standby."

"Where's that special response team?"

"No idea. What does the timer say?"

"Eighty-six minutes and fifty-two seconds."

"The guy leading the response team said don't touch anything. Also said it's good the timer is counting down, at least for now. Don't think I agree with that, but he said they will be there before too long."

"Hopefully, before it reaches zero. In the meantime, are we supposed to stand here with our thumbs up our nose and wait while…."

"Hold on, I'm on another line with him. Said he's almost to you and to clear an area in front of the monument for their helicopter to land."

"Yeah, right. He should know you can't get clearance for that. They'll have to land at an airport and drive in. Won't make it in time."

"That's what I said. Told me not to worry and pass the message along they'll be there in five minutes or less."

"I hope for his sake he gets clearance. Who is this guy anyway?"

"Said his name is Bob Onkst."

Guards stood thirty yards from the entrance to the monument as a flat-black helicopter set down squarely in the area they cleared. The only markings were subdued numbers on the tail. A small convoy of marked police cars and firetrucks with flashing lights and blaring sirens rolled up at the same time.

A grizzly looking man in his fifties dressed in black tactical BDU's stepped out of the chopper. A Glock Model 17 was strapped on his right thigh, and several magazine pouches hung from a utility belt.

He carried a black canvas tool bag and scratched a scruffy white beard as he walked toward the security officers. "Name's Onkst. Who'd I talk to a few minutes ago?"

One of the guards stepped forward and said, "Me. How'd you get clearance to land on monument grounds?"

"Doesn't matter, son. Take me to the device. What's the timer down to?"

The guard keyed the mike on his shirt epaulet. "What's the timer say?"

"Eighty minutes and twelve seconds."

"All right then, let's go boys," Uncle Bob said as he strode intently toward the entrance.

The guard set off at a near run to pass Uncle Bob and hold the double doors. He followed Bob in and led the way to the second-floor landing.

Georgetown, Md.

"BSOG-1, this is Washington PD, Unit 989. Do you copy?"

"Affirmative, 989, this is BSOG-1. What do you have?"

The Washington patrolman leaned over the top of the escape tunnel. "My dispatcher has numerous calls coming in of a white panel van rolling down a riverbank and into the river a couple hundred yards north of your location. Could it be your suspect?"

"It's entirely possible," Jake replied. "We'll head there as soon as we exit this sewer. Which way do we head?"

"Pipe empties into the river upstream and south of the possible suspect location."

"Very good, Officer. Thanks, and please keep me posted."

"Will do. Washington 989, standing by."

Ten minutes later, the BlackStar Ops group team entered the parking lot. "Get statements from everybody, and nobody leaves until I clear them." Jake said to the small cadre under his command.

"Jake, I got something," a rookie evidence tech shouted a few minutes later.

"What?"

"Ruts in the grass over here. You can see by the yaw of the tire marks where a van accelerated hard."

The tech pointed toward an area of flattened brush and small trees. "Looks like it flipped on its side and rolled into the river. Witnesses say it sunk within a minute or two. Can't see into the murky water to confirm anything. Local PD has a dive team en route. I've been told they can do swift water recovery in low visibility situations. Their dispatcher hasn't given me an ETA yet."

"Tell that dispatcher we need the dive team here ASAP. We need to confirm it was Yancy."

"Witness accounts say an older, stocky white male, covered in mud and limping badly got into the van. Who else could it be?"

"Not saying it wasn't him. But after all the tricks Yancy has pulled, we need to be sure."

"Roger that, sir. Looks like the dive team just got here."

"Kenny Saeger, Dive Team Chief," a muscular, middle-aged figure in black tactical pants and a tight t-shirt said as he extended a handshake. "You in charge here?"

"Matter of fact, I am. Jake Thomas, Team Leader. Thanks for coming. How long will it take to get your team in the water?

"They're suiting up while I debrief witnesses. I need to get a clear picture of what happened before I send my team in. With swift water, white caps, and zero visibility, it'll be a "Hellen Keller" dive."

"A what?"

"No visibility, and no sound. Basically, it's diving by braille, since touch is the only sense we'll have. We also need to tie off the subject vehicle, so it doesn't get swept downstream. Too dangerous to just jump in and hope for the best."

Jake frowned. "How long will all that take?"

"Not long, but it's better to take time

to recover the dead, versus adding more fatalities from my team."

"True. So, I guess we wait. Follow your original plan, Chief, at least for now."

"Will do. Now, if y'all will excuse me, I need to get to work," Saeger said as he turned and left.

***

Chapter 21

A two-man dive team entered the water less than ten minutes later to secure the van. A second team stood by geared-up and ready to act as a rescue team for the first...just in case.

The first team emerged after a few minutes and handed heavy ropes to dive team members who took up the slack and tied them off to three stout trees.

The first team disappeared into the murky water again. One of them carefully felt their way and entered the submerged van. The other diver stopped at the entry point as a safety precaution, in case something unexpected happened.

Several tense minutes went by until they surfaced and used the safety rope to pull themselves ashore. They stood in front of Jake dripping and wiping their faces with towels. "We have two DRT's inside the van...."

The rookie evidence tech scratched his head. "That's a new one on me. What's a "DRT?"

"Dead Right There. Anyway, we got a large Caucasian male with buzz-cut hair. There's also a smaller male with his face beaten to a pulp. He'll be a little harder to identify. If you're after evidence, we should probably recover them and the van at the same time."

"Damn the evidence," Jake commanded. "Bring the bodies out now."

"A word," Jay Johansen said as he pulled Jake to the side. "Careful there, Boss, this is no time to cowboy it. I know what you're thinking, but he's right. We would never run headlong into an unknown situation, and neither should they. Anybody who is dead will stay that way. We captured Yancy's men and recovered everything we came for, including Davis. We sure don't need to add to the body count."

"What the…what are you talking about, Jay?"

"This isn't a covert op. Just the opposite. The incident will more than likely show up on the evening news." He pointed to two news vans and a gaggle of reporters. "Media is starting to show up, so we might want to make sure we dot the eyes and cross the tees."

"Guess you're right. Thanks, Jay."

One of the dive team members returned from the equipment trailer with a body bag.

Jake held up his hand. "Hold on there. Saeger, could I have a word with you?"

"Sure. What do you need?"

"I've been thinking about what you said, and you're probably right. Let's pull the van up with the bodies inside.

Recovering the evidence may be vital to our investigation. How long will it take?"

"I have a wrecker standing by. We can have the van hooked up in a few minutes and winched out not too long after that."

Jake watched a dive team member taking notes and photos. "Documenting, I assume?"

"Yes, we've got to record every little detail. I realize we can't prosecute the dead, but this may be connected to other cases. One way or another, we've got to have all of our ducks lined up if we have to go to court. It's like any other case above or below water."

The steady whining drone of the tow truck winch stopped as the van reached the shore. Water cascaded from every opening.

A dive team member opened the driver's door and water gushed out for a few minutes. He started to enter the van when Jake stopped him. "This is a federal crime, so we'll take it from here."

The man began to object, but was cut short by Kenny Saeger, "Our work is done here, Hancock. Let somebody else do the paperwork for a change."

Jake extended his hand to Saeger. "Thanks for your help. Your dive team is one of the best I've ever worked with. I'll make sure my boss lets your people know that," Jake said with a smile. "The NSA Crime Scene Unit will take over from here."

Aaron Hagerston, Senior Agent in charge of the NSA CSU leaned in to examine and photograph the cab of the van, while another tech opened the passenger door. "No way we can do a quick ID through facial recognition."

"Why not?" Jake asked in a voice that conveyed his disappointment.

"Apparently wasn't wearing his seatbelt and bounced off the dash, the windshield, or both. Face is too smashed to get a good photo."

"Check his left leg for injuries."

"That he does have. Scraped up for sure. Also, what looks to be Russian Gang tatts, and a GSW to the leg."

"That does narrow the field. Get the body back to Fort Meade pronto. I need an ID as fast as possible."

"Will do, sir. I'll send it back in our Coroner's van with two of my best men, while I stay here with a tech to document the scene. I have a roll-off waiting to transport the subject vehicle, and we still need to search the factory for evidence. We'll be here for a while."

"As usual, Aaron, looks like you have it under control," Jake noted. "My team will wrap their work up here and return to our hotel to do reports. Maybe I'll see you in the morning."

"Bring strong coffee if you do. I have a feeling we'll be here all night."

Washington Monument

Uncle Bob followed the guards to the second-floor landing. "Thanks for removing the chain link fence, fellas. Would everybody please move back. I'm gonna need some room."

Uniformed police, fire, and monument security moved back a few steps, and watched the timer steadily count down.

"Okay, people, I just said I need more room," Bob said in a stern voice. The crowd moved back a few more feet.

"First step is to check this baby out. Somebody hand me a flashlight," Bob said to no one in particular. A police officer gave him a four-cell Maglite. Bob peered over and around the large metal box.

"Looks like they spot welded every nut and bolt. Somebody didn't want this baby going anywhere fast. Must not be any motion sensors in it though, or it would have gone off before now. Which makes sense, since elevators move a lot. How long has it been here?"

Nobody spoke until one of the monument guards cleared his throat and squeaked out, "It was first noticed about twenty-five minutes ago by a tour guide who reported it by radio. Nobody saw anything before then."

"Has there been any maintenance work done in the monument recently?" Bob asked.

The guard nervously looked around before responding, "Somebody made a notation on the Daily Events Log a few days ago that some guys came in late, worked on the elevator and left. Guards on duty weren't happy about letting them in after hours, but they couldn't get a hold of the Director. Repair guys had the right paperwork, so they let them in."

"When I'm done here, I'm gonna need to see that paperwork," Uncle Bob said. "And use gloves. We might get lucky and pull some prints off." Bob pulled a Geiger counter out of his tool bag. He turned it on, and it immediately started ticking fast, and loud. He set it down and dialed the satellite phone. "Jake, it's Bob."

"What do you have? Is it what we thought?"

"Sure is, and the countdown timer is running. The device is a flat black metal box about three-feet by two-feet by two-feet with warning decals all over it. Bolts mounting it to the top of the elevator have locknuts spot welded to keep it from going anywhere in a hurry."

"What do you think? You're the one on-scene."

"I think I need a vacation on the other side of the world."

"Wish I could help, but we're on a timetable. You're as good as me...."

Bob interrupted, "Don't know about that. Age is catching up, and I sure could use another pair of eyes."

"It so happens we just finished our op...."

"You get the subject?"

"No, but Joanna is safe. I'll fill you in later."

"That's great news, but back to business. How soon can you be here?"

"Hang on a second. Chopper pilot says less than fifteen minutes. Already has the coordinates and flight clearance."

"Guess you figured I might need help. See you soon?"

"Boarding the bird as we speak."

***

Chapter 22

Upriver From Georgetown

"Like I told you earlier, Mister Yancy," Wild Bill spoke above the engine noise. "I'm here to rescue you and take you to a safehouse." The middle-aged operative wrapped a shivering Yancy in a heavy blanket. "Once we get further away, I'll treat those wounds. I have a change of clothes for you too."

"Tell me your name," Yancy shouted.

Wild Bill stared upriver without answering. Instead, he spoke into a satellite phone in a quiet voice he knew could not be heard above the throaty roar of the twin three-hundred-horse outboard motors.

"Everything okay?" Morgan's voice came through clearly.

"Yeah, Boss, it's going just like you planned. I'm headed back to the marina with the subject. He'll need a doctor to treat a through-and-through to the leg. Nah, didn't hit any major blood vessels. Spent some time in the water, though. Came real close to being a human popsicle. Also seems a little confused about the rescue, but I'm sure you'll straighten him out. See you in less than an hour."

The cabin cruiser motored on at mid-speed for another ten minutes. Wild Bill figured they were far enough way to take the time to treat Yancy's wounds.

"Let's go down into the cabin and get you cleaned up. I put the boat on low idle and we're mid-river, so we can take care of those wounds."

Wild Bill helped Yancy hobble down the three steps into the interior cabin of the boat. He kept an eye forward for anything in the river, and to make sure they were not veering toward shore.

"Here's a towel and some dry clothes."

Yancy struggled to get out of the wet and muddy clothes and dry himself. "I... I...I am better with dry clothes. *Спасибо,* uh, thank you."

"You're welcome. It's my job to take care of you." Wild Bill handed Yancy a cup of hot coffee and looked for signs of shock.

After a few minutes, Yancy managed to get the dry clothes on and wrap a fresh blanket around himself. "You work for Morgan, yes? Where is safehouse?"

Wild Bill stared straight ahead and slowly moved the wheel from side to side to maintain course.

Washington Monument

"Guess we need to figure out how to remove or open the device without turning the National Mall into a nuclear waste zone,"

Jake whispered to Uncle Bob, as he joined him on the second-floor landing.

They stared at the box they knew contained the small-yield nuclear device known as the BlackStar System.

"Man, oh, man," Bob replied. "All the training and simulations we've had, you'd think I'd be ready for this. But I gotta tell you, the pucker factor is through the roof."

"I know how you feel, so let's get started. We need to drill a hole in the top and drop the pin hole camera in to check for booby traps. If it's safe, we cut it open. What's the timer down to?"

"Fifty-nine minutes and thirty-seven seconds."

"We have time, so let's go slow. Can you clear the area?"

"No problem." Bob turned to the crowd of emergency responders. "We need to clear the area, please." Blank stares, and nobody moved. "Listen up, people. You don't want to be within a half-mile of here if this thing goes off. We got this, so please clear the area."

One of the police officers spoke up, "I think I can speak for all of us when I say we are in this for the duration. Besides, you're gonna need a hand getting the top of the box off. You can't do this all by yourself."

"Thanks, and while that means a lot, most of you have families, so think of them." With that, a murmur went through the crowd and some slowly walked off.

Uncle Bob turned back to the box, grabbed a cordless drill, and went to work drilling a hole in the top. He paused almost ten minutes later and used a shirt sleeve to wipe sweat from his forehead. "My hands are cramped so hard I can barely hold onto the drill."

"Need a hand?"

"Would you mind, Boss?"

"No problem. You can spell me after a while."

Aboard The *Star of the Bay*

"Where is emergency kit, money, weapons, and medical supplies from van?" Yancy asked in an urgent voice.

"Back deck of the boat," Wild Bill replied. "I put them there after I loaded you. You can crawl out and check if you want to."

"Maybe, I will do so later. Again, I ask who are you? Where do you take me?"

"Call me Bill, or Wild Bill if you like. Guess you're suffering from the effects of the icy river. We're going to a safehouse. Until then, you might want to sit back and take it easy. I'm here to protect you."

Yancy scowled at Wild Bill. "How long is trip?"

"We reach the marina in about fifteen minutes. I'll treat your wounds before we leave the boat. It'll take a half-hour or so after that, depending on traffic."

Yancy sat back and shivered uncontrollably. He sipped hot coffee as the boat gently rocked back and forth. With the muted hum of the motors droning on, it was easy to sit back and relax, even if only for a few minutes.

Washington Monument

"Aargh, that's the second broken drill bit in less than five minutes," Jake said. He wiped his forehead with his sleeve. "This isn't good. I forgot how solid they built these things."

"Maybe because the last time we saw one was our initial training," Uncle Bob replied. "Should I send for more bits?"

"No, I think it's almost…all right, just broke through. I'm extracting the drill bit now." He blew metal shards away from the opening. "The pinhole camera is in."

A light source mounted on the camera illuminated the interior and a monitor showed the inner workings of the bomb.

"Okay, I'll move the camera from one side to the other so we can see everything. The bad guys mounted two pressure plate actuators to the top of the box at each end. I can get around them both to cut a hole in the center of the box."

"I'll extract the camera now." Jake carefully pulled the cable out of the box. A heavy collective sigh was heard from the nearby witnesses.

"How about you take a breather?"

"Sounds good," Jake said as he stepped back. "It's all yours, and where's the restroom?"

"The head's that way. While you're gone, I'll use a circular saw to cut a rectangle in the top to avoid the pressure plates"

Jake stared intently at the monitor. "Start about eight inches from each side, and a foot or so from the ends. I'll be right back."

Bob slowly cut through the top, making sure not to lean or push the saw downward with any more pressure than needed. "I'm making my fourth cut now."

He motioned for one of the guards to come closer. "Officer, would you very gently use those needle-nose pliers to grab the far end. When I cut through on the last side, I don't want the plate to fall onto the device."

The officer's hands were visibly shaking. "Easy son, it's a walk in the park."

Uncle Bob made the fourth and final cut and went very slowly in the last half-inch.

The officer used both hands to hold the top of the box and slowly eased it away.

Jake returned from the restroom at the same time and leaned over the cut edge of the device. "I was afraid they'd tamper with the BlackStar System, and I was right. Looks like they added a timer and some sort of internal security system. Everything else matches the schematics we studied in training."

"Well, I guess that part is good," Bob replied. "What's next?"

"We need to determine how it was modified in order to disarm it. Let's take a moment to study it."

"Not too long, I hope."

"Hey, take all the time you need. We have at least forty minutes before it blows up in our face."

An audible gasp came from the bystanders on the landing. Bob's eyebrow went up. "I believe your sense of timing needs a little work, Boss."

"Yeah, never was my strong suit. Let's start with the trigger to make sure they didn't put a jumper lead in it."

"Whoa, good catch, because they did. I can see at least one wire that shouldn't be there. I'll check further to avoid more surprises. And there you go, winner, winner, chicken dinner. They installed a jumper wire before the timer to bypass it straight to the trigger. You know in case somebody like us wanted to spoil their party."

Jake bolted upright and exclaimed, "You're not the only one with a surprise. Knuckleheads added a couple more wires further down in the device. Almost didn't see them."

"Can you see where they go?"

"Looks like the length of the device. One even comes back to the timer. No clue what it does, but I'm pretty sure it's not good," Jake said as he scratched his head. "By the way, did you locate the lead ball with the surprise inside?"

"First thing I looked for. No added wire there, which is a real blessing."

"It should have color-coded wires. Have they been tampered with them?"

"Son of a gun…"

"I don't like the sound of that."

"Didn't notice until you asked, Boss. Two of the soldier joints have been worked on by a pro. Either the wires were switched and resoldered, or made to look that way in case we noticed it was modified."

"I have to admit they did a top-notch job. The solder is an even bead, and the wires are tightly crimped with pliers. Still doesn't tell us what they might have done, though."

"Wait, I see speckles of solder on the base of the device. The work is good, but not original. Wonder what that might mean?"

Jake forcefully exhaled. "Could be one of two things. If they switched the wires and we cut one it could set off the device. Or cutting one in a Hail Mary move to try and bypass the timer could also set it off. Either way, we need to be careful, or we are screwed."

"Along with a million innocent bystanders. Of course, there is a third option. Could be they unsoldered and re-soldered the same wire just to mess with us."

"You have a twisted mind, my friend. It's one of the things that makes you so good at this."

"Gee, thanks, Boss, I think."

***

Chapter 23

Aboard the *Star of the Bay*

Wild Bill dropped the cabin cruiser to idle as they approached the marina. He expertly docked and left the cabin long enough to tie off. "Let's take a look at the gunshot wound." He gently cleaned and bandaged the wound.

"You are also doctor?" Yancy asked.

"Me? No, but I've spent enough time in places where there was no medical help. Had to take care of wounds or die. Like I thought, it's a through-and-through. That's a good thing. I'll get antibiotics from a doctor I know. As for your foot, looks like somebody raked your shin pretty good. How hard did they come down on the top of your foot?"

"Very hard. I think maybe is broken."

"We can take care of it later if it doesn't heal fast. I have a cargo van parked at the far end of the lot."

"How do we get money and weapons to van?"

"Piece of cake. I've got two of those huge coolers with wheels used by sport fisherman. We can pull them to the van. That'll also explain your limp."

"Okay."

Bill helped Yancy up the steps to the aft deck of the boat. He used the motors to hide them while they loaded the coolers and shoved them up onto the dock.

The men tried to look as nonchalant as possible while pulling the large coolers toward a nondescript white delivery van.

"Hand me pistol," Yancy spoke quietly as they approached a marked police car.

"What? No, nothing stupid. We're just two fishermen taking our catch to the parking lot." He put a hand on Yancy's shoulder, and said in a loud voice, "Hey, look, a pretzel cart. Let's grab one and something to drink."

Bill smiled as he pulled Yancy to the edge of the lot while keeping himself between his charge and the parked patrol car.

Yancy peeked around Bill's large bulk. "Policeman stares at us like he knows…."

"No, he doesn't. He's eating a sandwich in a quiet place, like I used to do. He only looked at us casually. Couldn't care less unless you draw his attention. Now eat your pretzel and keep your back to him."

Wild Bill glanced toward the marked Washington DC patrol car and waived at the officer. The officer stared for a second, waived back and took another bite of a fish sandwich.

Washington Monument

"What's the timer down to now, Bob?"

"Thirty-two minutes, twelve seconds."

"Ok, we've gone through everything we can up to this point. Time to cut wires."

"And that, my friend, is the tricky part. We've narrowed it down to three that go to the timer."

"We can't forget wires may have been switched on the housing unit for the...."

"Lead ball thing," Bob interrupted. "I know. You want me to cut the wires?"

"No thanks. I'll take responsibility in case something goes wrong."

"I don't think we have to worry about facing the music if it goes wrong. It will all be over in a flash." Uncle Bob grinned.

"Well, thanks for that encouraging remark. Guess I'll cut the white wire, then."

Jake slowly moved the cutters so one side was on the wire. He pulled it slightly taut. Beads of sweat dropped onto the device, even though the elevator shaft was cold.

A quick snip was followed by a resounding pop. Numbers flashed by as the timer spun down with incredible speed.

"Holy crap," Bob said out loud. "What's happening?"

"No idea, but we're down to our last option, the Hail Mary. Gotta be the blue or red wire. Our best guess is all we have now."

The group of men standing on the landing inhaled as one. Jake looked over at wide-eyed faces staring at them. "What do you think Bob, blue or red?"

"Hey, it's your call, but what do you think the guy who rigged it would do? What color should it be versus the color he decided to make it? Blue for safe, or red for danger?"

"Red sky at night, sailors delight. Red sky at morning, sailor take warning. So, I'm going for the blue."

Jake was mesmerized for a moment as the timer raced through two minutes. He placed the cutters on the blue wire and slowly squeezed the handles. He switched to the other wire at the last second.

"Red," he shouted, and snipped the wire. The timer froze at nine seconds, and slowly faded.

NSA Contract Hotel, Bethesda, Maryland

Jake looked around his hotel room at the BSOG team. "We've been down a rough road the last few months, but we recovered the nukes and Joanna. Every single one of you was instrumental in completing the mission. Lots of hardship and lost sleep, but thanks to dedicated teamwork, we accomplished what some would say was an impossible task."

"I couldn't agree more," Uncle Bob added as he raised his glass. "Here's to our team and a monumental effort, no pun intended."

Jake put his hand on Uncle Bob's shoulder and surveyed the room of smiling faces. "I think it was intended. I also think we should drink up and relax for the rest of the evening. Keeping in mind, we have reports to write tomorrow and equipment to maintain."

A symphony of groans filled the room.

Jake waved his hands up and down. "But that's tomorrow. Tonight, we party."

Cheers slowly subsided and were replaced by typical party chatter. Small groups of people talked, laughed, and became emotional as they remembered lost comrades.

Jake pulled Joanna into a corner and held her face in both hands. "Thought I'd lose it for sure, thinking about what Yancy and his men might be doing to you." He shuddered and stared at the floor.

"I'm all right. They didn't treat me all that well, but they didn't abuse me or anything. I tried to escape, but they were too well trained. I knew from the bottom of my heart you wouldn't stop until you found me." Tears welled up in her eyes and she hugged him as hard as she could.

"Oof, can't breathe."

"Wimp. Sorry, but I want to hold you like this forever."

"Be really hard to work or eat, and I don't even want to think about going to the bathroom."

"Eww, that's gross. Let's change the subject. How do you thank Yancy got away?"

"Not simple luck, that's for sure. It was a well-orchestrated setup that guaranteed he'd have enough time to get out of the warehouse. He had transportation and a driver, and that points to an organization with unlimited resources. Which tells me there's a good chance some of his people are still running around free."

"So, how do we find them, and who will lead them with Yancy gone?"

Jake eased the embrace and stopped smiling. "Uh, we need to talk about that. After what you've been through, I'm not sure you should be involved, at least for a little while. Wait, don't push me away."

"Then don't try to shut me out."

"I'm not. I am trying to protect you."

"By smothering me? I'll go crazy if I can't be in the middle of things. You, of all people, should know that."

"What, have you become an adrenaline junkie or something?"

"No more than before, but I really need to catch the man who held me prisoner."

A scowl darkened Jake's face. "You know that revenge can really screw with you, right? Remember the old saying, 'Before you set out to seek revenge, dig two graves.'"

"It's not just about revenge. He needs to go down to protect the one I love."

"The one you love? Who would that be?"

"You, dummy. He told me he wants you dead."

"That's not the first time I've heard that, and I don't understand. What did I do to light such a fire under this guy? I don't even know him."

"No, but one of the men guarding me said you killed Yancy's brother."

"What! Where? Don't you think I would remember killing his brother?"

"Unless he was disguised, or if it was a highly classified op."

"Well, there were a few of those early in my time in the Air Force. I was on loan to an alphabet agency on some ultra-classified ops. Most of the subjects were approved targets, so their identities were known. Wait, now that I think about it, there was an op in the PI we had to evac in a hurry. I suppose it could have been one of the bad guys I eliminated out of necessity."

"Whatever it was, it looks like you have a serious target on your back," Joanna said, as she buried her face in his neck and hugged him even tighter.

Uncle Bob turned to Jay Johansen on the other side of the room. "The team needs to blow off a little steam. They probably feel like they've been beaten like a rented mule. I know I do. That's right, I am one whupped pup. Think I'll head back to my room for some sack time."

"I understand, Bob," the third-in-command of the strike team replied. "Glad we're in Jake's hotel room, though. I can't imagine what the Director would say if these conversations went on in a public place."

Uncle Bob laughed, "I imagine he'd stroke out, and with good reason. You can't say anything about nuclear devices without raising an eyebrow or two."

Both men smiled and took a long sip of their drinks.

Liquor flowed and after a few hours, the party slowly died. One by one, the team said their goodbyes.

Jake and Joanna were finally alone in the wee hours. He looked at empty bottles, cans, half-eaten pizza, and snacks. They sat side-by-side on the couch. Her head rested blissfully on his shoulder with her arms wrapped around him. A smile painted her face until she fell fast asleep.

"I'd better get some sleep too, my princess." Jake eased out of her grasp and stumbled to the closet for a blanket. He gently wrapped her up like a Christmas present and stood watching her sleep.

After a while, he swayed and staggered toward the bed, fell into it, and pulled the covers over him.

The incessant ringing of the cell phone jarred Jake awake. He fumbled around the walnut nightstand, knocked the phone off, found it, and answered the call with a grunt.

"Bob, if that's you, I'm gonna kill you…."

"No, Jake, this is John Banner. Did I wake you?"

"Huh? Oh, Director…sorry, thought it was Bob." Jake tried to clear his hazy mind.

"Sorry to bother you in the middle of the night, but no time is good for bad news. I will give you a minute to wake up."

"I'm ready, so what's wrong?"

"I just talked to the Asset Protection Team. They inventoried everything you confiscated from Yancy's men. We collected more than we thought we would, but we're still missing a nuke."

"A nuke? No, that can't be right. How could it be? There were several crates, and I was sure it was in one of them."

"So did everybody else, including me. APT went through every crate several times and came up empty-handed."

Jake exhaled sharply. "Yancy must have squirreled it away somewhere. I really wanted him, but I wanted the nukes more."

"We all did. After all, our job is to protect the devices. And no, before you try to take the blame, it was not your fault. You shot him, tracked him, and he went into the river in the van. Although we need to have Forensics give us a positive ID on the body.

We also need to redouble our efforts to find the missing nuke."

"I'll get the team together and let them know, Director."

"Hold off on that for a little while. Let's give the team a chance to recuperate before we break the news to them."

"You're the boss." Jake yawned and looked at the glowing numbers on the bedside clock. "Look, I don't mean to be rude, but I need to get a little more sleep than the few hours I've had. We're going to wrap up paperwork in the morning. Are we still meeting with you at 1600?"

"Absolutely. See you then."

***

Chapter 24

NSA Director's Office, 1600 hours

"Nothing like rescuing a fellow agent and preventing the destruction of a revered national monument," John Banner said as he raised a glass of Kentucky bourbon from a bottle he kept in his desk for such occasions.

"Not to mention dismantling a deep-cover spy operation," Uncle Bob added.

"Maybe not completely, but at least we put a serious dent in it," Jake said. "Unfortunately, I have a feeling their tentacles go deeper than we can imagine."

"I will not argue with you on that," Banner said. "We need to continue searching for other operatives who may have slipped through our grasp. I also have information that cannot leave this room. I should have mentioned it before, but one of the wounded mercenaries wants to make a deal."

"I didn't know any of them lived," Uncle Bob said.

"Officially, he didn't. Turns out he was wearing enough body armor to survive with minor wounds. I have him stashed away in a safehouse."

"Let's hope he's more than a run-of-the-mill thug who can provide some useful intel," Jake said.

Banner leaned back in his chair. "If what he says is true, he has got a ton. He also claims to be secretly working with another operative we know, Jack Morgan."

"No way, really?" Jake said with a surprised look.

"Yes, really. In fact, I have Mary Benson running down some of his claims."

"Mary Benson? Haven't seen her in a month of Sundays," Uncle Bob said.

"Mary was promoted to head of our European Desk, and spends most of her time buried in intel analysis. You might want to stop by and say a quick hello while you are here."

"I sure will."

Banner turned toward Jake. "You are being awfully quiet. Something wrong?"

"No. Well, actually yes. There are a number of things on my mind, but I don't want to ruin the moment."

Joanna leaned over, put her hand on his shoulder and quietly said, "Go on, tell everybody."

"Yes, please share your concerns, if you do not mind," Banner said.

Jake began slowly, "Well, we got most of Yancy's team...."

Uncle Bob broke in, "Most? I was under the impression we got all of them."

"And that's the way it looks at first glance," Jake replied. "But Yancy is known for complex planning and tends to pre-position operatives ahead of time. His escape is proof of that, even if it went wrong. I mean, there's no way to know for sure, but I would guess he was already setting up his next operation. You know he wasn't going to finish this one and just walk away."

Banner rested his elbows on his desk. "Those are all good points. Which means we still have work to do, especially with what we talked about last night."

The team exchanged puzzled looks.

"What do we need to do?" Banner asked.

Jake paused. "Not much we can do except monitor communications, collect intel, and see what pops up. I say that because I think he is connected to a larger organization that will continue to throw a lot at us, even if he is really gone."

"Can't say I disagree with you on any of...."

The Director was interrupted by an assistant poking her head in the door. "I know you didn't want to be bothered, sir, but I think you'll want to take this call."

"Thanks, Kathy," Banner said as he answered the call with a simple, "Banner." After a few questions, he thanked the caller before he hung up.

The Director whistled and addressed the group, "That throws a whole new light on things. Forensics finished the autopsy, and the body in the van was not Yancy."

The team responded with stunned looks.

"What now, Director?" Jake asked.

"You are the leader of the team. Any ideas?"

"We need to regroup and formulate a new plan to track him down. But first I need to meet with the team and collect my thoughts. How about the two of us meeting tomorrow morning for a private discussion?"

"Fine by me. I'll clear my schedule and see you at 0900."

"I'll be here with bells on," Jake said with a grim look. "And I won't rest as long as Yancy is a free man."

****

From the authors:

We sincerely hope you enjoyed the story and would ask a favor.

Please go to your favorite review site and post an honest review. Some examples are *Amazon.com, Goodreads.com, Bookbaby,* or *Facebook.*

We do not have a huge promotion budget, (most small publishing companies do not,) so word of mouth is our best advertising.

Your support will be appreciated more than you can imagine.

■■■

T.c. Miller and J.A. Schrock

T.c. Miller, and J.A. Schrock

■■■

BlackStar DC

A preview of

BlackStar Consortium

Book Six in the BlackStar Ops Group Series

Consortium Headquarters, Switzerland

"Doctor, why do you stare at the lab next to us so intently?" a technician asked the older balding man in a lab coat.

"I observe the crate that was placed in it yesterday," the perplexed scientist mumbled as he stared through two sets of lead-glass windows.

"Are you concerned, Doctor?"

"Somewhat, I must admit. The windows allow an open view that reduces a feeling of claustrophobia. The design also permits unfettered observation of adjunct teams at work. Which means we may spot anomalies quickly and report danger to those who manage the laboratories."

"I assume you refer to accidents?"

"Precisely. The design allows us to safely conduct experiments with nuclear and biohazardous material."

The technician responded with a puzzled look, "Do you mean bioweapons?"

"Do not fear, my young colleague. We have not worked with bioweapons for quite some time. I do not recall the last time thermonuclear devices were present. We are well protected. In point of fact, only the Commissioner's office is more protected."

"Like you, Herr Doctor, I do appreciate a safe work environment. Still, if you do not mind an observation from me, you seem unusually worried about the device in the lab next to ours."

"For good reason. The device they uncrated reminds me of thermonuclear weapons I created for my mother country.

Although, the control panel is considerably different, and is in English. I also do not recall blinking red lights. Dear mother of God, I now see why. A timer has activated. Please, quickly sound the alarm."

"I am, as we speak."

A siren and klaxon wailed to a nearly deafening level. The technician spoke into an intercom, "This is Laboratory 14. A timer on the device in Laboratory 12 has begun counting down. It displays twenty-three minutes and fifty-eight seconds."

"Calm yourself," a voice on the intercom replied. "It is undoubtedly an event of little consequence."

"What if it is something far more dangerous? What if it is a precursor to an impending detonation? An investigation should be initiated. We need help now," he screamed into the intercom.

"I see, and your point is well taken. We have dispatched an emergency response unit," the voice on the intercom said.

The sound of men running in the hallway could be heard even through hermetically sealed doors.

Two scientists in Laboratory 12 pressed sweaty palms and faces against the electrically locked door that refused to release them.

The doctor and lab tech in Laboratory 14 watched helplessly with heartbeats pounding in their ears. "What are they doing? Why do they not deactivate the device?" the young lab tech asked the doctor.

"It appears they do not know how, my young colleague. Observe their expressions. They appear to be desperately screaming into radios and gesturing wildly. We need to leave here posthaste."

Both men scrambled feverishly to open the sealed door. They punched control panel buttons that did not respond, since wrong codes were entered in the frenzied attempt to leave. Computer security systems automatically blocked exit.

The young technician sank to the floor and whined, "We are doomed."

"You may be correct."

They heard a security team leader in the hallway scream into his radio, "Get me the Commissioner immediately. I need to speak with him."

A haughty voice came out of the speaker, "You must take a more civil tone with me when requesting my assistance," an aide to the Commissioner replied. "Screeching your request will not endear you to me."

"A timing device on what appears to be a bomb is counting down with less than nine minutes left. Is that important enough to scream at you?"

An older voice broke in, "Team Leader Alpha, this is the Commissioner. What is so important that you must interrupt a meeting to speak with me?"

"Thank God, it is you, sir. A device has been activated in Laboratory Twelve and is counting down. I require the code to disarm it."

"Counting down? That is curious. Who activated the timer?"

"I do not know, Commissioner. Please tell me you have the code to stop it. Otherwise, we may all die."

"Control yourself, man. I see no reason to panic. You must simply follow established protocol. Furthermore, you should have thoroughly investigated to uncover who activated it before disturbing my busy day. Discover the identity of the person who committed the error and call me when you are certain. I must also admonish you to show more respect when speaking to me or my subordinates."

The team leader stared at the silent radio and addressed the room in a voice loud enough to be heard over the alarms, "Find somebody who has the code to disarm the bomb."

Every security agent in the room began a desperate attempt to locate the code. Shouts into radios, telephones, and intercoms produced no results.

The realization seemed to strike all of them at once. An eerie silence settled over the lab complex as the enormity of the situation struck home.

The timer counted down.

***

Made in the USA
Middletown, DE
22 April 2022